ALAN SHIVERS

Europea Halls 3

Copyright © 2024 by Alan Shivers

All rights reserved. No part of this publication may be reproduced, stored or transmitted in any form or by any means, electronic, mechanical, photocopying, recording, scanning, or otherwise without written permission from the publisher. It is illegal to copy this book, post it to a website, or distribute it by any other means without permission.

This novel is entirely a work of fiction. The names, characters and incidents portrayed in it are the work of the author's imagination. Any resemblance to actual persons, living or dead, events or localities is entirely coincidental.

Alan Shivers asserts the moral right to be identified as the author of this work.

First edition

This book was professionally typeset on Reedsy.
Find out more at reedsy.com

I want to dedicate this book to all the readers who have stuck with Oliwia and the world of "Europea Halls". I am sincerely grateful for all of you!

Acknowledgement

Here it is, the final part of the slasher trilogy. It's actually been more emotional than I thought it would be, saying goodbye to a world that has meant the world for many reasons.

To my parents, family & friends: thank you so much for your continued support and faith in me. The last couple of months have been hectic, so I appreciate you all taking my mind off things and checking in on my mental health when self-doubt crept in. I love you all. Can we go on a little holiday now?

To Matt Seff Barnes, my cover designer: I appreciate the time, effort and patience you've put into creating these rebranded covers. I know I have a specific taste, but I am glad you are understanding of that and I will forever promote you to other authors!

To Amanda, my editor and proofreader: when I ran out of synonyms or decent sentence structures, you've helped out to save the day. Thanks, not only for your work, but also for being a massive indie horror author supporter and a kind soul.

To all of the podcasters and interviewers over the past months who have shown interest (still blows my mind): you truly help spread the word and visibility. Your work is so selfless, it is really touching! Sharron, the Core Four, the Creepy Podcast, Jim from Horror Movies and Shit and everyone else - you rock!

To my two fellow slasher authors Sarah Jules and Emerald

O'Brien, I am so glad we found each other! Please have a look at their books, they are beyond scary!

ARC reviewers: you people are the best! Thanks so much for reading the book and promoting it, I know you didn't have much time to read it this time around, so a massive thank you to all of you. To the six early reviewers who have made the effort to write a blurb for the hardcover: I wouldn't have been able to have a finished book without you!

And last but certainly not least: thank you to all of my readers who have joined me on this trip. I appreciate the messages, the reviews, the likes and everything in between. Reach out to me on social media and let's have a chat!

And now: let's head into Europea Halls one final time.

Chapter 1

SASKIA

Something about this entire night feels off. Do you know that hunch you get, when your senses signal you to stay alert, even though there's no actual danger around? That's how I've been feeling for the last couple of hours. Like I'm on edge for no reason. Unrest sits deep down in the pit of my clenched stomach, gnawing its way further inside. Maybe it's just this crowd. I've never been good with crowds, but somehow I allowed Jelena to convince me to come to Bloody Louis. She said it would be "the best time", celebrating New Year's Eve in one of Brussels' biggest clubs. Now granted, it is quite nice spending my evening in an old Gothic church, full of people dressed up to the nines: champagne, sparkles, the whole shebang. The mistake was just the two of us coming here, alone. The rest of our friend group from the movie club had all gone back to their home countries for the winter holidays, so Jelena thought we might as well celebrate together. And then she disappeared on me. No idea where she went, she isn't answering any of my messages. She's seen them though, and not responding is very unlike her. Maybe I should walk around one more time to check if she's on the other side of the dance floor.

"Are you alright?" A tall man in a perfectly-fitted matte black suit asks me. He isn't just tall, there's a whole lotta muscle underneath those clothes. I bet he's Italian, that slicked back long hair isn't the typical Belgian look. He's a fine looking specimen. *Now* we're talking.

"I'm fine. A little lost, I suppose." I bat my eyelashes coyly and instantly cringe at myself. Ah well, I can at least have some flirty fun tonight.

"I figured, that's why I came over. What's your name? Mine's Fabrizio." Of course it is; a walking stereotype. But a handsome one at that.

"Saskia, a pleasure." He shakes my hand and gives me two kisses. Yep, definitely Italian.

"So, tell me Saskia, why are you all alone on New Year's Eve?"

This man is quite direct, but I probably do look a little sad standing here by myself. "My friend ditched me and it was supposed to be us two tonight, but I have no idea where she ran off to. I checked the toilets, but nothing."

"Sorry to hear. Can I get you a drink?" His voice is smooth and calm; it eases away the tension. He pauses for a second. "You are over eighteen, right?"

"I am, I'm twenty-two." Bit of a weird question.

"I'm just asking 'cause I know some underage people have snuck in."

"How would you know?"

"I recognise some of them." He looks away and glares at some girls by the dance floor. That's an odd thing to say.

"How do you- ?"

"I work at Europea Halls."

"That private boarding school in town?"

"Yep, that exact one. I'm a guard there." I'm not surprised,

CHAPTER 1

judging by his physique and demeanor.

"I've always wanted to see that place." It became quite famous after all the murders two years ago. No pictures of the interior ever made it into the news and believe you me, I've tried to find them. I've only ever found outside shots.

"Why is that, Saskia?"

For some reason I don't like it when guys I've just met say my name like that. Feels like some forced job interview. But I'll give him a pass, it beats being on my own.

"It's just, everyone in Brussels knows the place, but unless you go to Europea, no-one has ever set foot inside. It has this element of-"

"Mystique?" He smirks. I'm still deciding whether he's confident or arrogant. My 'cocktail goggles' mightn't be the fairest of character readers.

I smirk back. "If that's how you want to put it. I'm a sucker for interior design and Brussels has all these tucked-away gems that are impossible to visit."

"*Almost* impossible." He winks at me.

"What are you getting at?"

He slides his hand into his trousers' pocket and dangles a key-card in front of my face, as if I'm the luckiest prize winner of the night. "Nothing is impossible. I can get us in if you want a free tour."

I hesitate. That sounds like the exact kind of random adventure I'm looking for, but I don't know the guy. "How about that drink first?"

"Coming up. What can I get you?"

"Aperol Spritz, please."

"Ah, you know your drinks. Italian." Jackpot, told you so. "Although it is a summer drink, I'll let it slide." Another wink.

3

He's a bit of a sly fox from what I can gather, but I admit: I'm not mad at the attention I'm getting. Not exactly boyfriend material, but I'm here for a good time, not a long time.

Fabrizio – that name, really is right off a sleazy, spicy romance book cover – has taken me to a private balcony in the VIP lounge, overlooking the dancing masses. He seems like the kind of guy who would have access to these places and pride himself for it. He is already starting to piss me off a bit with his constant references to materialistic and exclusive things. Yes, I've seen your watch. No, there's no need to point out the brand. Maybe I should just go home instead.

"How's the Spritz?" Wow, a question. Did he tire himself out talking about himself?

"It's lush, thanks."

"You seem a bit bored."

"Was that a question or an observation?"

"A bit of both. Perhaps it's time for your guided tour."

Bed and Netflix or murder hall tour. I'll go with the latter.

"I'm up for that. Won't there be other people around?"

"No, the halls are closed each year during the winter and Easter break."

"Has it always been like that? From what I remember in the news –" Ah crap, he hasn't mentioned the murders yet, what if he knew anyone that got killed? No-filter blabbermouth is in full action, thanks booze. His thick eyebrows rise. "The news. So you know what happened."

"Doesn't everyone?" I ask as nonchalantly as possible.

"Fair point. Anyhow, you're right. The halls used to be open all year round, now they close down over the breaks. There was a huge protest from the parents. All of a sudden they had to

CHAPTER 1

take care of their own kids during the holidays, imagine." He chuckles.

"The horror."

A kind smile erupts from his full lips. It's the first time I see a crack behind the facade. I'm sure it can't always be easy, working for those rich diplomat families. He probably has to put up a front so those Eurocrats take him seriously.

"The worst. In other words, we have the halls to ourselves tonight. Just you and me." I'm not sure if that excites or scares me. A bit of a mix.

"So you weren't lying when you mentioned a private tour?"

"I never lie." The gravitas in his voice sounds forced. There's the facade again.

I gulp down the rest of my drink, in an elegant fashion obviously (minus the spillage on my silk dress) and grab his very toned arm. "Well then, lead the way, Fabrizio." Two can play that game.

He unlocks the stately main doors and puts his key-card in front of the scanner. I rub my arms as January's chill cuts through my way too thin evening jacket. A beeping sound and a little green circle follows. I'm actually getting into Europea Halls tonight. I want to squeal with excitement like a teen, but I keep myself composed. The Halls are a place of class, I can't let him see my dorky side. Not tonight anyway.

He opens the doors, switches on the hallway lights and signals for me to come through. The anxiety I felt earlier swings back, full force. I feel tingles running down my spine. I have to admit, I'm not here just for the interior, morbid curiosity is definitely part of it, too.

I'm instantly impressed by the grandiose main hall. It's a

shame he told me I can't take pictures here. Oak floor boards, the massive Renaissance - or Rococo? - paintings, the massive chandeliers - this place reeks of absolute power and wealth. So this is how the one percent lives in Brussels. A pang of jealousy hits, but at least I can be a voyeur for the night. I take off my jacket, put it on the coat rack and step deeper down the hall.

"So, what do you think?" His eyes are full of excitement now; he's way cuter like this.

"I mean -" I twirl around the main hall a couple of times, my echo hitting the high ceiling. "What can I say? This place is incredible." Incredible, yes. Creepy, yes. Also, the halls being vacant doesn't exactly help.

"Isn't it? I often pinch myself. I used to be a bouncer in some rough clubs in Brussels, so when there was an opening for a job here, I jumped at it." He is adorable.

"It can't have been easy to get a job here."

"It's not, they're very selective." He straightens his chest - hello, pecs - and looks like a proud Boy Scout.

"Could you show me where the toilets are? I need to have an empty bladder." Gross, that wasn't sexy at all. "I require full focus to experience the private tour."

Fabrizio smiles, he is so much more himself (I think so at least, don't actually know the guy) since we walked into the halls. We're on his turf here. "Sure, follow me." He takes me by the hand, subtle, and leads me to the toilet.

"Gender neutral?" I ask, surprised. These old institutions don't always have the reputation of getting with the times.

"Well, in a way. These are the girls' halls. But the staff's toilets are gender neutral, yes."

"Girls only halls? What century are we living in, for real?" A little test for him.

CHAPTER 1

"I agree. These binary divisions are way too outdated." Look at that, he passed.

I stare into the mirror. How are even the toilet mirrors a work of art? The golden frames are full of intricate ivy-like details and the light bulbs glow with a soft iridescent hue. The sink is elegant too, the little tab is the cutest I've ever seen.

I take a quick selfie, I'm sure he wouldn't mind. My hair doesn't look nearly as straight as it did at the beginning of the night, but I'll just go with the blonde surfer-chick look for tonight. The stain on my maroon silk dress is way more obvious than I thought it was too. A little disheveled, but then who isn't past midnight on New Year's Eve?

Maybe I should try a selfie from this side, I could -

Ping.

I shriek and drop the phone into the sink, then quickly grab some tissues to dry it off. Maybe Jelena has finally gotten back to me. Let's have a look.

Unknown Number: *Welcome to Europea Halls.*

What? Who wrote that? A tightness forms around my chest. Unease shoots through me. I jet out of the bathroom and into the hall, where Fabrizio is still waiting for me.

"I know I'm not entirely sober here, but - just to be sure - I didn't give you my number, did I?"

He frowns and tilts his head slightly. "Not yet, no. Is that a smooth way of you asking me to ask you for your number?"

"I - what? No! Look." I show him the message. He takes a prudent step back. The confident man is nowhere to be seen right now.

"That's strange." He ponders for a while, pacing through the main hall. "Did you text your friend you were coming here?"

"No, I didn't. I didn't tell anyone. Did you?"

"No, nobody." He looks at the ground, deep in thought. "Actually, I did tell some colleagues I would crash here tonight."

My mind is spinning. "Your colleagues, okay but still. How would they get my number?"

"A prank?"

"It's not even funny." I say dead serious.

"Those guys have access to things you wouldn't even believe."

"Those guys? Meaning, you as well?"

He coughs a little awkwardly. "I suppose so. I didn't send it though, I swear."

"On what?"

He looks into my eyes again. "On pasta. And Spritz." There's that smile again. Fine, I believe him, but this is still creepy as hell. I think he can tell I'm not at ease here. Not one bit.

"Do you want to leave? I'd fully understand."

My rational brain tells me to get the heck out of here, but I'm far too curious to walk out now.

"I mean, I should. But I'm also really intrigued about this place. And I've got you as protection, right?" I wink at him, flushing away my fear with some flirting.

"Absolutely. They call us Arms, the girls at the dorms."

"Arms?"

"Yes." He takes off his coat, throws it down on the staircase, and flexes his right arm, stretching his tight black shirt dangerously thin. It looks like the seam is about to pop.

"Oh. It looks like I'm safe." That's all you can say? Jelena would smack my head. In all honesty, it's a super bad move to flex like that in front of a girl. It helps though. Just in this situation, of course. In any other I would've left by now. Totally.

"You are, I know this place inside out. So let's forget about whoever tried to prank you and move on. Here-" He grabs my hand and gives me a soft kiss on the cheek. "Let's start with the paintings. There are paintings of different pagan gods from all over Europe, which I think is quite cool."

"No overly Catholic paintings for once, that's refreshing." I exhale slowly and try to hide the biting fear that still lingers.

"Exactly, the girls are being watched over by just about any European deity you can think of."

We stroll past the bombastic looking gods and scan the faces of Brigid, Thor and Frigg. Fine, I am reading off their names on the golden frames, I admit it. I walk up to one of them.

"Saint Paulus? Doesn't exactly sound pagan."

"I guess they threw in some good old Catholic ones for good measure."

I walk closer to another painting. "This one doesn't look that protective. Who's this?"

A fierce man with white eyes and white wavy long hair is staring back at me. He is standing in what looks like the sea or some sort of lake.

"That right there is Leviathan."

"Levia-who now?"

"Leviathan. A demon of envy and sin. He helped Lucifer out with some deal if I remember the story correctly."

I swallow slowly. "Lucifer? How is that supposed to be comforting for students?"

He scratches his temple. "Yeah, okay, maybe not the best example here. Not quite sure how this even made it into the hallway gallery. It's a recent addition. I spotted it the day after the halls closed down for the holidays and did a bit of research. Anyway, let's move on."

"With a little drink, to stay hydrated?" I could use some extra liquid courage, these halls exude something far darker than I could've imagined.

He squeezes my hand. "Well, alcohol is not allowed on the premises. But Arms here knows better." Don't call yourself that, please. "Come with me."

"Where to?"

"The kitchen."

Fabrizio unlocks a cabinet at the back of the kitchen and pours me a whiskey. He didn't even ask if I like it, but the stronger the better right now.

I take a couple of sips and feel the burn mellowing out the dread in my head. "So, is it true? Did the girls get killed in the kitchen?"

His dark eyes penetrate mine. "Here? No, where did you hear that?"

"Oh, I don't know, there were so many stories going around at the time."

"From what I remember, two of the girls fled into the kitchen to take the lift there." He points at a shabby service lift at the other side of the kitchen.

"Why did they go in there?"

"Not even sure how they knew about it, it's normally off limits for students."

"Naive much?" I poke him, but he doesn't laugh. A heaviness appears to take over his posture.

"They went up to the library on the top floor."

CHAPTER 1

"There's a library in here too? Of course there is. What happened there?"

"The whole showdown. One of the killers was almost killed in there. Actually, the real showdown happened in the gardens." Somehow that doesn't interest me as much. The interior is way more appealing.

"The library, though, sounds eerie."

"Oh, it is." He pauses. I think I can spot some sadness in his eyes.

"Can I ask you something?" I tread carefully now, 'cause I don't want to upset 'Mr. Arms'.

"Sure."

"Did you know them? The victims?" I take another sip of the whiskey, hoping it isn't too insensitive to ask.

"I wasn't working that night, I had the morning shift. But I did. I knew all of them. They were all lovely girls."

"Wait, so that means your colleagues? Some of them got killed too, didn't they?"

"They all did." There are most certainly tears in his eyes now. A bit of a mood killer, these questions of mine. I can't stop myself though, finally someone who knows more about all of it. "I was close to those guys. I took some time off after to get my shit together. It wasn't easy coming back."

"I bet. Respect for coming back in the first place."

"And those girls. It's a big school, as you can tell by the size of this place, but they were all very well-educated, polite young women. It's horrible what happened to them."

"Oliwia is the only one who survived it, right? I mean, after this past summer in Budapest."

He nods gently. "The only one from that friend group who is still alive."

"Are the media lying about that?"

"What do you mean?"

"Nobody knows where she is. Allegedly."

"I don't know about that. I can imagine her family buying off the media so they'd have some peace. What I *can* tell you is that she doesn't live in these halls anymore. Not a clue as to where she's hiding."

"The sole survivor. I wouldn't want to be around here anymore either." This place is giving me the creeps, just thinking about what has happened here. I actually feel a bit guilty lurking around like a murder-hungry tourist. A cutting silence hangs between us.

"So, do you want to see the library? It is quite stunning." As if we can just switch back to interior design after that entire conversation. Something still pulls me in though.

"Sure."

"Let's take the lift."

"That old thing?" I hate lifts with a passion, if you can even call that tin can over there a lift.

"It's stronger than it looks."

I smile. "That makes two of us." I clench up my fists and force myself to walk in.

As the doors close, he takes my hand and looks deep into my eyes. Oh, he knows what he is doing.

"How many girls have you taken up to the library, Casanova?"

He protests. "Excuse me? You're the first. I'd get fired if I ever did this during the school year."

"And during the holidays?"

He looks down at his feet. "Fine, you're the third." I'm not

CHAPTER 1

sure if I should appreciate his honesty or get out of the halls. "But, by far, the most beautiful one."

I smirk.

"And smartest." He goes in for a kiss, but I'm far too tense in this shaky lift, so I duck. "Not here, maybe the library."

He cracks a smile. "I know just the place."

I gasp in disbelief as the lift doors open; there's no way schools have actual libraries like this. What kind of a derelict old school did I go to? "You're kidding me." I glance at the gorgeous late-Gothic stained glasses and the dark wooden ceiling panels covered in Cherub paintings. I walk towards the aisles covered with dusty books and let my fingers glide over centuries of knowledge. I'm sure these are all first editions, too.

My hand stops moving. I'm startled. I check what's happening and notice he has put his hand on mine. I turn around and face him. "Is this the place then?"

"Almost." He steps closer and I feel his body heat permeating my cold silk. He takes my other hand. "I'll show you. Come." For a moment I think he is about to try to kiss me again, but he pulls me away from the aisle instead and guides me deeper into the library. We walk past several shelves until we reach aisle L.

"Here we are."

I look around the aisle, I don't get it. "What's so special about this spot?"

"It's called Lovers' Lane. Aisle L."

"You can't possibly be this corny?" I poke him again and this time he does laugh. We lock eyes as he approaches me. He caresses my cheek and leans in for a kiss. I close my eyes and feel his tongue gliding inside my mouth, my entire body instantly reacting, goosebumps all over. He pushes me closer and I can feel his heartbeat racing against mine. Say what you want about the guy, but he knows how to kiss. Promising start.

"Your heart." I touch his muscular chest.

"What about it?"

"Are you nervous?" I wink at him, pretending I'm not.

"Of course I am, look at you." He goes back in for round two and I happily comply. I leave my hand on his chest as it feels rather comforting and also, it doesn't hurt to squeeze those pecs.

His tongue tastes oddly metallic. He could've taken a mint first, rookie mistake. Hold on, it's more like a thick liquid. I pull back to look at him. His face is in shock.

"What's wrong?"

"Saskia. I'm-" he tries to speak through the blood that begins to run out of his mouth. What the actual - My stomach clenches again; there's that feeling.

A sharp pain hits my hand. I look down and notice the blade of a rusty machete piercing through Fabrizio's chest and the palm of my hand. Dark blood runs down, dripping onto the wooden floor boards of the library.

I scream and stumble backwards. What is happening? I clasp my injured hand in my other and try to stop the bleeding, but the cut is too deep. Fabrizio's eyes roll up as I see the machete stabbing through his forehead. His blood spews all over my face and I shriek. I don't think he fully understands what's happening either. He doesn't even shout or say anything. His entire body starts shaking for what feels like forever before he collapses onto the floor.

Then I see it. That mask. It's the one from the massacre, cracked with age and full of old blood stains. My heart skips a

CHAPTER 1

beat. That text message, he knew we were here. The masked figure holds up the blood-soaked machete and walks in my direction. "Leave me alone, you freak!" My heart rocks inside my chest, clinging to life.

I ignore the biting pain in my hand and run out of aisle L and into the main hall of the library, with the killer at my heels. I jolt towards the lift, but the doors are closed. The machete slices through the air, flying past my head and into the lift door. I scream and head for the stairs instead, as the figure struggles with the blade, which is lodged deeply into the metal door.

I run down the first flight of stairs before I hear a clunking sound; he's got the machete out of the lift door. He's following me again. My mind is running a million miles an hour, trying to think of a way out. The only way out is the main door. Now. *Keep going. Or hide, should I hide?* He's too close, he'll know where I am. If I remember correctly, the library is on the seventh floor, so I'm on the fifth floor by now. Just continue down. I hear the sound of the machete swooshing past me, barely missing. "Get away from me!" I look behind me and notice how close he is. *Keep going, don't look back.* I sprint past the landing of the fourth floor, sweat-beads trickling down my forehead and into my cleavage. I feel sick, my heartbeat pulsating like mad in my throat. Just three more floors. I up my pace and urge my legs to move faster.

A sharp pain rips through the left side of my back. No. Please no. This can't be real. I've been struck by the machete, falling down onto the landing of the third floor. I feel the blade twisting inside me, the agony excruciatingly unbearable. I shout into nothingness, hoping for the halls to bring solace or help even.

But I'm alone here. Alone with the killer.

He pulls out the weapon, scraping past my intestines. Everything hurts. *Everything.* He grabs my back and turns me over, towering over me with his legs spread. "What do you want from me? I didn't know any of those people." But I know that's a lie. I know Oliwia. And Karla. And some of the others, too. He doesn't need to know that though, neither did Fabrizio. No response. I kick up my left leg and aim for the groin, 'cause what other option is there? I hear a muffled grunt as he loses his balance and drops to the side. *This is my chance.* I kick him in the ribs and make my way down the stairs. No running anymore, I'm losing too much blood. I move as swiftly as I can, but I'm painfully aware of how slow that really is.

My phone buzzes in my pocket. I quickly grab it. The killer hasn't moved yet, judging by the silence surrounding me.

Unknown Number: *Tell me where Oliwia is and I'll let you live.*

He knows. He knows who I am, and my connection to the others. How? I look up and shout: "I don't know where she is, I swear! Nobody does!" An unnatural intestinal movement makes me double over, the agony almost blinding me. I can't handle this much longer. "I haven't heard from her!" No response. But there's sounds again. Slow steps down the stairs spring me into focus. Don't give up now, you're already on the second floor.

The door is open. Room 214, Ingvild's dorm room. Oliwia told me. No, I'm not being dumb about this, he obviously wants me to go into the room. I continue my path down towards the main hall, but the figure is picking up speed and is running down the stairs now. I look up and see the black shoes casting a haunting shadow over me.

CHAPTER 1

One more floor. I'm getting out of here. The wooden staircase creaks beneath us, crying out into the night. I see him, the mask popping up around the corner, swooshing closer. "Just let me go, I don't know where she's hiding!" But it doesn't slow him down. My right knee is shaky and my legs turn to jelly. Feet, don't fail me now, as Lana del Rey would say.

There, I made it to the main hall of the ground floor. I can see the massive wooden doors on the other side. *You've got this, hold on. You can make it out.*
Go.
The killer jumps towards me.
The blade slices through my shoulders. I fall down onto my knees, my left hand barely stopping me from flopping all the way down. I vomit liquor and fear out onto the boards. He kicks me in the back, my back and my knees cave as I drop into my own vomit. I cry out in pain. He's got me.
"Tell me where she is!"
It takes a moment to click. That voice coming from behind the mask. *There's no way. There's absolutely no way.*
"You? I told you, I really don't know. Please let me go. I haven't seen her."
I'm being turned around once again, facing the mask. "And you never will." The voice is full of pure hatred.
A smaller knife is pulled out of the long overcoat and glides underneath my right eye. I shudder. With one swift move, my eyeball is severed from its socket. I hear it tumbling down the hall, like a morbid marble. I want to shout, but I'm too shocked. The knife pushes underneath my left eye and I feel it cutting its way inside my head. My vision vanishes, just like that. I notice blood trickling inside the cavities. Realisation hits, there's no

way out anymore.

"Stop, you know me! Please!" is ringing inside my head, but I can't get the words out anymore. Another stab, from the machete this time, I think. The blade goes into different parts of my body, faster with each hit. Then it hits my throat. And again. Deeper this time.

"You know me."

Chapter 2

ERIK

What, what? My head is pounding, who on earth would call me this time at night? It's - I check - almost 4AM. I sit up in my bed, the room engulfed in darkness. I guess a lot of people are still up, it *is* New Year's Eve after all. I'm proud of myself for making it past midnight. Parties, no thank you.

It's Jelena. Drunken slur incoming?

"Jelena? Why are you-?"

"Have you seen your sister?"

"No, wasn't she supposed to be out with you?" A hint of worry sets in.

"She was, but I lost her when I went to the toilet. It was super busy in Bloody Louis, and I can't seem to contact her. It's *so* not like Saskia to just up and leave though."

My woozy mind is thrown into focus. What has happened to my sister?

"How long did you look for her then?"

"Over an hour! I got really stressed out, it was just the two of us going out tonight, so I was on my own. She's not over at your place, is she?"

"At mine? No, she never crashes here. Have you gone to her

apartment in Schaarbeek?"

"I did. Took an insanely expensive Uber and banged on the door for ages, but nothing. I'm sorry to wake you up, Erik, but this feels off."

"No, I'm - I'm glad you did. I appreciate it. Where are you now?"

"I've just arrived back home. What should we do?" It sounds like she's close to tears. I hold mine back too. She's right, this feels off, way off.

"You've done what you can for now. I'll ring my parents, and I'll go over to her apartment, too. My mum has a spare key to Saskia's place. I'll update you the moment I find out more, deal?"

"Deal." She pauses. "You've always been a good brother to her. She loves you, you know?" Why is she speaking like this? She isn't dead. Is she? A lump forms in my throat, making it hard to speak. All I can say is "I know. I'll be in touch."

I lay down in bed again for a second to fully register the content of the phone call whilst staring at the shadowy ceiling. What should I do first? Go over there? No, I should call Mum, but she'll freak out and perhaps Saskia is just drunk and sleeping over at a friend's place or at some random dude's. The lump enlarges. What if it's something bad, though? *Don't go there, she's fine.*

I hear a faint tapping coming from underneath my bed. My body immediately freezes and I hold my breath. Perhaps it came from outside. There it is again, only a slightly bit louder. It appears metallic. My eyes are wide open, seeing more nuance in the greyish menacing shadows on the ceiling. It's too dark in here to look for something to protect myself with, but this

CHAPTER 2

is my room, I know where I've put my taser. I knew I'd need it one day after everything that had happened. It's in the bottom drawer of my desk, just across from my bed. *Get up, don't just lie there.*

More tapping, actually more like scratching sounds this time. What if it's just a bug, or a mouse? That phone call put me on edge, there's no need to -

Thud.

I feel a small push, like someone nudging me in the back from underneath the mattress. This ain't no mouse.

Thud.

Another push, this time more violent. I snap out of my frozen state and sit straight up in bed. This call - Saskia missing - the noise underneath my bed - I need to leave, now.

A swooshing sound directs my gaze next to my left hand. A glistening knife protrudes from the bed linen. I scream, jump up, my lungs forcefully pumping air and courage into my system. I bolt for my desk, it's jammed. I glance over my shoulder and see a tall hooded figure with - I knew it. That mask. I'm cornered in the dark. My shoulders tense up and despair fills my entire nervous system. I shout for help, hoping my neighbours will hear me. Why is he just standing there?

"What do you want?" A small tilt of his head, barely noticeable, is the only response. The weapon is the only thing gleaming in the dark. Then the figure jumps in my direction, knife firmly in hand.

Chapter 3

OLIWIA

I inhale the salty sea breeze as the sun sets deep into the Mediterranean. The sky still holds firmly onto its warm reddish glow with dispersed specks of clouds only vaguely hinting at the time of the year. It's the first day of the new year and a rush of emotions comes rolling over me, rhythmically following the breaking waves. It's that day when people make their resolutions for the upcoming year, full of courage and naive hope. That day when people are forced to sit at a large dinner table with their relatives, even if they'd much rather sleep off their hangovers. Not for me though.

My mum squeezes my hand. I look at her from the corner of my eyes and I can tell she wants me to make eye contact, but it's easier to stare at the sinking sun. Still, it is a comforting feeling having both of my parents here with me. We sit with our bare feet plunged into the sand, wearing light sweaters, and hold onto a version of family that could still work for us, somehow. Local Spaniards pass us by with thick coats and scarves on. Some glare at us as if we're absolutely mad for not wearing the correct attire. It's nineteen degrees, people, chill. What I've learned from these past five months in Spain is that locals dress according to the month, not the actual weather. The

CHAPTER 3

moment October hit, they all switched their entire wardrobes, even though it was still sweltering hot outside.

Playa de Calblanque is my favourite beach in the region of Murcia. It's not like I've seen that many beaches since we've forcefully been moved here into hiding under police protection - more about that in a moment - but this one takes the top spot. We've only gone to the non-touristy places to make sure we'd stay away from crowds and (according to Dad) danger, which I do appreciate. Just nature, time to ourselves and time to heal. Even though it's only been a couple of months, I'm convinced I'm further along in the grieving process than I was after a year in Brussels. I recognise the different phases this time around. It didn't get easier, but I understand the patterns now.

The first few weeks, my head was in a very dark place, I won't lie to you. I had lost everyone that mattered, barring my parents. My girlfriend, my best friend. I can say their names though, I *want* to say their names: Karla and Ingvild. One way or another I clawed my way out of the void. I kept thinking of them and how much they'd kick my ass for crying and not leaving my bedroom. No more pushing feelings and anxiety down. Hypnotherapy - yes, Vera has a full schedule thanks to me - is allowing me to be okay with being raw and vulnerable. A big part of dealing with PTSD on a daily basis is not being very coherent with my way of thinking and having fragmentary memories all jumbled up, but I can live with that. So if I jump a little from topic to topic, bear with me. I'm trying. I have been trying.

You're probably wondering what happened after Budapest. Let me try to fill you in. As the police - my favourite, I know - were closely following up on Balazs (oh right, I need to talk about him as well later) and me, there was no escaping their help this time around. The moment my parents and I landed in Brussels, the local force was waiting for us at my dad's private landing strip. They knew about the text message. About Lovers' Lane in Europea Halls. They couldn't drag me back into that boarding school, everything was still too fresh at that point, so my dad joined the police corps. In all fairness, he didn't have much of a choice. I told him I don't trust the police and that I was too scared of going back there myself, so he went along without even a hint of hesitation when I asked him to. Nothing. They rummaged the entire halls, Miss Raven even closed down the building for some days so the police could do a thorough search for any signs or clues as to what that message could refer to, but nothing. I wasn't surprised, but I did hope some sort of finality could've been reached. Instead, the ominous ending, the *Third Act* is looming. It still is, I'm very aware of that. This isn't over and, at some point in time, I'll be pulled back into Europea Halls, much like Laurie Strode was confronted by good ol' Myers thirty years after the first "Halloween" film took place. For now, I'm here. At the beach in Spain.

I look over my shoulder for a second and Lukas waves at me like the eager-beaver he is. I don't wave back, cause I can't be arsed. When the police unit in Brussels didn't believe I was safe, they suggested a police protection system in which we'd go into hiding. Well, suggest would be the euphemism of the year. I tried to wriggle my way out of that straitjacket of a life, but my parents and I ended up agreeing on having one police officer with us at all times. Originally there would've been five, could you imagine? I'm still not happy with this and I'm sure it comes as no surprise that I don't trust Lukas one bit, but I got tired of my parents' pleading and crying. I don't have the

CHAPTER 3

energy to fight every single case anymore. I need to pick my battles in life. I've had plenty.

What else has changed? Oh right, school. I no longer go to school, I'm nineteen now anyway, but I do follow two different online courses. The first is an architecture course, specialising in Art Nouveau. That one's for Ingvild. The other course, and I still can't believe I'm saying this, is EU law. Yup, for Karla. I decided that a proactive way of keeping them near me is by studying the subjects that made them who they were. When I look around the mansion on top of the mountain that we're staying in now, I take in details I never would've noticed without the art course. I want to look through Ingvild's eyes when I see the beauty of buildings. The European law one is trickier. I'm still a bit bored, but I imagine Karla sitting next to me in front of my laptop, slapping my lap whenever I doze off. I miss them. So much, it hurts my entire being. It is all-encompassing grief. They're everywhere. Every song I hear, every series I try watching before realising I can't focus, every smell - The tiniest of details brings them back. But you know what? That's how I want it. I don't want to push them away. So I've learned how to bring back the other girls, too. Vintage shopping with my mum - whilst thinking about Alzy, Ayat obviously being on my mind a lot now that I live close to Valencia - or planning little hiking trips for my parents the way Marieke would've. Now that I'm saying all of this, there's a part of me that is proud of myself. I'm still here. They're not. So I owe it to them to keep on going. Alright, you've caught me at an okay moment, looking at the sunset and taking in all the crisp looking nature around me, but still. I'm damn proud actually.

Anything else for now? Balazs, right. He's the only one

who has my new phone number. Going into hiding meant not using social media, which I'm absolutely fine with. It's been a welcome detox. Balazs is worried, bless him. He's always worried. I think it's because he doesn't have a twin sister to look out for anymore, I'm the closest thing. We talk about three, maybe four times a week I'd say. He's my only friend. I haven't made any friends here. It's not exactly the Erasmus experience other European people my age go for and you'll catch me dead before I call Lukas my friend. He's only thirty something, but he appears much older, even though he is not in uniform. I suppose he has to exude a sense of authority or whatever it is, but yeah - not my buddy. I try to be polite to him, but I often fail.

The only semi-friend I've made is Tanya, but that's largely because of my mother's interference - I mean social-skills. Tanya's parents are the owners of the Real Casino de Murcia, which is this gorgeous old money type Moorish casino. The architecture is stunning, Ingvild would've loved that place. It's very elite, in other words, very mum. She knows people everywhere, it comes with the territory of being a Countess. So when she met Tanya after some social event, she absolutely had to introduce her to me and, naturally, my mum thought it'd be a great idea to try to play cupid between Tanya and I.

"Hey Liv." I swallow hard. Nobody is allowed to call me that except for my parents and Balazs. It's Tanya. She gives me a slow, gentle peck on the cheek and before I can say anything, she sits down next to me on the sand. Her radiant black skin catches the last traces of sunlight left of the day. Her black dreads are tied back, showing off her elegant shoulders. She might be wearing a thick coat, but somehow the fabric hugs her figure tightly, the way it always does. I look over at my mother who has ever-so-smoothly scooted a bit further down the beach, leaving a place for Tanya to sit next to me. My mum's angry eyes are burning into my dad's, it makes me smile. She is trying to signal him to give Tanya and me some space, but the poor ol' man is clueless. So we sit here, my dad to the left of me and a smiley Tanya to the right. And yes, Lukas behind me. This is as natural as it gets in my life nowadays.

Chapter 4

BASIA

I am trying to signal Mirek to give Oliwia some space, but you could hit that man with a hammer before he gets social cues. IQ is more than blatantly there, EQ though - a whole different story. My darling needs this, she deserves it. She hasn't truly had the chance to connect with people her own age since Budapest. If she so happens to be gay, well, what can I say? The matchmaker in me couldn't stop myself.

I met Tanya's parents at a social gathering in the Real Casino de Murcia. I was invited to come over for a charity event, and even though I am usually rather reluctant these days to be the guest speaker, it is terribly difficult to say no when there is a good cause behind it. Can't remember what that cause was, in all honesty, but we did raise a stellar amount of money. Mirek was apprehensive of me going, but I had Lukas by my side to ensure safety. He cleans up quite well, that young man. The number of gazing eyes I had to shake off with him in his tailored suit next to me, it was almost too much. Spaniards do have a weakness for blondes, so I've been told. Those luscious locks and olive green eyes would make anyone's head turn. Anyhow, Tanya's parents are from the same social circle, so that always

CHAPTER 4

helps. Decent people who don't hunt you down for your money are hard to come by these days. They graciously showed me around the entire gem of a casino, adding in lovely details of its eclectic style. It was erected in 1847, the exact same year my ancestors had built their castle in Krakow. Almost an eerie coincidence, that. When they presented Tanya to me, I could instantly tell she would hit it off with Oliwia. The same love for film and gusto for life. Well, the gusto my girl *used to* have for life would be the more accurate thing to say. Perhaps she could bring out that spark again, that vigour I know is there, deep down. If there is anyone who deserves a tabula rasa, it's my darling.

It hasn't been easy for any of us. Leaving behind our estate in Brussels, even the staff, to move to a rather modest villa in a small city in Spain was quite the transition. The things you do for love. I understand the necessity for safety and for going into hiding, but luckily Lukas had assured me that a little outing now and then would still be possible. I knew there was no press allowed at the casino, so that convinced me in the end. We all need it, as it can get quite suffocating being stuck inside a temporary home, not knowing any of the neighbours or local culture. The traveller in me had to be tempered, not going out every single day, exploring our new environment. But this isn't an extended holiday. This is our life now.

We don't have the faintest idea how long we'll be living here, but according to Lukas we'll be able to go back home once the killer has been caught. And this is where it all gets so complicated. We all know this won't ever become our home, but we're still trying to lay down some sort of foundation here at the same time, 'cause who knows how long this phase of our lives will last. It all feels a bit like a fever dream. Also, the heat can be highly unpleasant and if there is one thing I detest it is dressing down just for the sake of the climate.

The past months have been more than a test for our family. Even though the police had promised us that the birth certificate and adoption papers were forged, the unease in Oliwia had lingered. One day she knocked on our door in the morning, fiddling with her hair - which thank the lord is back to natural dark blonde. I'm all for expressing oneself, but that pink did look a tad bit pedestrian - asking Mirek and me to take a DNA test. The paranoia had gotten the better of her. At first I felt furious and deeply upset that my daughter could even question the legitimacy of our parenthood, but the hurt in her eyes said it all. She just wanted some form of safety, in whichever way possible. So we did. Once we had proven we were Oliwia's birth parents, something in her changed. Not for the better though, in my opinion. I don't think she allows herself to fully comprehend what has happened to her and her friends. She is taking classes, going on walks, doing all the proactive things. But I know my daughter, it's a way for her to flee the grief that is stuck deep within her core. After those tests, she hasn't mentioned LeBeaux's name, not even once. Whenever I do bring up the past, she changes gears and shifts to a different conversation. She does mention her friends and Karla a lot, but only in a positive light. I have this uneasy feeling that at some not-too-distant point in the near future she will crash, all those losses being too overwhelming.

The absolute worst thing for a parent is this: being powerless. I desire with all my might for my darling to get better and to build up a life again, but I am so utterly and completely powerless. I

CHAPTER 4

listen to her, I take walks with her, we even laugh sometimes, but none of it is enough. I want to take away her pain, let her live again. I've had a good life, she's too young to be living with this sort of heartache. It's not fair. We've done everything in our might for the past nineteen years to raise her the right way, having a good support system and the luxuries that we can luckily provide her with, but what does all that matter when your daughter's innocence and happiness has been taken away so brutally, so unjustly?

And then there's the other thing. What if this isn't actually over yet? What if *whoever* is still out there and knows where we are and comes for her - or for all of us? I'd like to drench myself in naivety and trust Lukas to handle things, but that hasn't worked out too swimmingly in the past. One day, I hope we'll all be able to sleep again at night, not jumping up at every nocturnal sound. One day we'll all be safe again, surely.

Chapter 5

TANYA

If Liv's mom thinks she's being subtle, she is sorely mistaken. Her eyes look like they are about to pop out of her skull, looking sideways without moving her head. It's kind of funny actually. Not exactly what I'm used to, but this girl seems worth it. There's something incredibly intriguing about Oliwia. Obviously, she isn't too hard on the eyes, but there's so much more beneath the surface. This is the fourth time I'm seeing her and the way she coyly smiles at me melts my heart. I do hope I will get to have some one-on-one time soon without her entire entourage, but it's understandable after all she's been through. She hasn't told me a thing about Budapest or Brussels, but my parents (and the news) have filled me in enough to know that this will take time. Well, guess what, I'm not going anywhere. I've met plenty of flaky girls over the past months and to meet someone who has actual depth and maturity is a breath of fresh air. Of course it's not as carefree or flirty as dates usually are, but I can hardly blame her - or her parents and that bodyguard of theirs. My dad is a little too eager for me to "court" - as he so awkwardly puts it - Oliwia, smelling the opportunity of climbing the social ladder even further. It's not about that for me. Nor should it ever be.

CHAPTER 5

"You chose a good day to see the sunset." I blurt out, not quite sure why.

"Did I? I mean, it's gorgeous, but so far they have all been lovely. I don't think rain is legalised yet in Murcia." She pulls a small smile.

"Oh, it is, but when it rains people go mad here, legit. So many car accidents, you wouldn't believe it." Stop being a snooze fest Tanya, just ask her what you came here for. "Listen, Liv -" Her smile fades. "It is okay for me to call you that, right?"

"It - I mean, yes sure. I'm just not used to it any more. But, of course."

"Oh, right. Sorry. Did that trigger anything, or -"

She looks the other way, off into the horizon. "No, it didn't. It's fine."

I don't know how to read this girl. Doesn't help that I'm 'Miss Clumsy' around her either. I don't want her to think I'm walking on eggshells here, but I kind of am. I don't want to hurt her or say anything dumb, but by doing so I say dumb stuff all the time.

"Okay. Well -" She turns back to face me, her face slightly contorted. I think she's biting back tears. Great job Tanya. "I wanted to ask you something."

"Go for it." She forces a smile again, but I can tell she's only being polite. Maybe now is not the right time. Don't make a big deal out of it, you're over-analysing.

"Go on then, what's the question?" She nudges me with her elbow, a bit of a spark coming back now.

"I wondered whether you'd be interested in going to the cinema with me tomorrow night."

Her eyebrows lift high with surprise. "Oh, I see. That sounds cool. I'm not sure if my parents will -"

"It's fine darling, go and have fun! I have discussed the matter at hand with Tanya's parents!" Her mother shouts out. Great, she's obviously been eavesdropping. I'm not mad at her though, this might be the little push she needs. Thanks for the helicopter-parenting, Basia.

"Mum, for real? Have you been listening in on our entire conversation?" Oliwia yells back.

"It's - it's the wind, it carries the sound right to me." She wears an apologetic smile.

Oliwia shuffles closer to me, ready to whisper something in my ear. Electricity seemingly ignites as I feel her breath on my skin.

"Sorry about my mum. She means well, she's been in momma-bear-mode ever since - what happened. I feel so embarrassed."

I whisper back, tingles and sensations heightening by the second. The sea breeze carries her sweet perfume. "Don't worry about it, you can tell she loves you. It must be hard for her." I pause, gathering the courage to reapproach the previous question. "So, tomorrow night?"

"The thing is, I will probably need Lukas to come with, which isn't ideal. I'm not allowed to go anywhere on my own - you know, public places and all."

"Oh no, it's not like a regular cinema. We have a home cinema at my place in Murcia. There are also guards walking around the grounds, so you'll be fine. Plus-" A muted cough escapes my mouth. "I will protect you." I wink at her and instantly regret it. Luckily Oliwia doesn't look too turned off.

"Oh, you will? I see how it is." She winks back at me, she *actually* winked. Should I wink again? Tanya, behave.

"I will ask Lukas to drive me to and from your place then. I'm

CHAPTER 5

sorry about all of this, by the way."

"Don't be. I can only admire your strength and everything you've been through, Liv." I pledge to myself, no references about her past tomorrow. Unless she *wants* to talk about it, of course.

"I appreciate that. Right, what time then?"

"How about nine? I can prepare some tapas for movie night."

"Sounds amazing! What are we watching?"

"I'll let you decide. You are definitely more of a movie buff than I am, as much as it pains me to admit that." We both smile, relief takes over. Finally a moment of spontaneity.

"Sounds good, give your address to Lukas and he will text you with my movie of choice."

It is still so odd she won't give me her number, but maybe she's not allowed to, who knows. It almost feels medieval, "courting" her - yes, Dad - through her guard. Pigeon post, anyone?

"Sounds like a plan!" I pat her on the back, another lame move, and stand back up. Where's my liquid courage when I need it? That's it, next time I'm drinking a Tinto de Verano before seeing her. "See you tomorrow, Liv!"

Chapter 6

BASIA

This is smashing, I don't believe I have seen Oliwia smile like that in months. As Tanya walks off, politely waving at us all, I stand up and move closer to her again. She stays seated, so I decide to position myself between Mirek and Oliwia.

She slaps me on the knee.

"What on earth was that for, darling?"

"For being so nosy!"

Mirek chuckles.

"What are you laughing about, then? You weren't exactly Mr. Read-the-room either. You stayed right there, our daughter needed space to -"

"Space? Like you gave her?"

"A mother is allowed to look after her child, Mirek."

"Guys, please - not this again. It's fine, both of you. Treat me like an adult next time though, please, I felt like I was a teenager again."

I lift my arms up in surrender. "Fine, fine, I will give you all the space you ask for."

"Write that down somewhere." Mirek adds and smiles at Oliwia.

This is almost normal. This conversation, as if we're a regular

CHAPTER 6

family.

"I will. Anyway, she's nice. It'll be fun to hang out with her tomorrow, without all of you breathing down my neck." Oliwia turns her back and glares at Lukas. "No offense. Well, maybe a little."

The poor man must be used to it by now, but still, he's only doing his job. "None taken. Well, maybe a little."

Mirek laughs again. He's been a fan of Lukas since day one. My husband has never been a man of many words, one liners are more his thing. But, in some odd turn of events, Lukas and him often have deep talks together. Whenever I come near, the conversation fades. Utterly frustrating.

"The thing is –" Oliwia continues. "I don't want to lead her on."

"How so, love?" Mirek ponders.

"Dad, come on. It's barely been half a year since – since Karla passed away. You can't expect me to throw myself at the next girl that comes along." She looks at both my husband and me, eyes full of pain.

"Oh darling, of course not. But there is no harm in watching a movie with a pretty girl."

"Isn't there, though? It feels like cheating. That probably sounds ridiculous."

"No, it doesn't." Mirek replies warmly.

"She meant the world to me, you both know that. I loved Karla, a lot. I still do. Tanya is nice, but there's this guilt eating away inside of me at the same time."

"That's a very humane reaction to have, Oliwia." I'm positively shaken. She is so open with us right now, so we need to grab the bull by the horns. "And I am incredibly proud of you for vocalising your emotions to us. This is good, this is right. *You* being honest with *yourself*. That's growth, darling."

A faint smile forms on her face. "You sound like Vera sometimes. Maybe it's just how people your age talk."

"People my- pardon? Vera is at least five years my senior."

"Posh mature people then, better?"

"Splendid, thank you." We all laugh again. It still baffles me how we can go from high to low back to high in a matter of minutes. This is the way our conversations have been over the past months. Raw emotions, all jumbled into a claustrophobic feeling of alienation due to no longer living at home. "Well, at least tomorrow you can speak with another immature young person then. Perfect mix."

"Burn." Mirek has my back when Oliwia challenges me. Not always, but when it matters.

"On that positive note -" Oliwia takes her purse and shakes off the sand. "I say it's time we go home. It's getting a bit nippy out now anyway."

Oliwia and Mirek walk ahead of me in silence, arm in arm. A lovely sight to behold. Lukas is walking behind me, until he gently pulls at my sleeve.

"Lukas?"

"Basia, can I have a moment?" His energy is off, the nervousness in his voice apparent.

"Sure Lukas, what is it?"

"Not too loud, Miss, I wanted to tell you this first before we decide what to do with Oliwia."

I take a deep breath. None of that sounds even remotely positive. "Excuse me? What is going on?" I try my hardest to whisper while glancing at my daughter and Mirek walking in front of me, the breeze caressing their hair - they look so

CHAPTER 6

peaceful. I don't want to ruin that moment.

"I have received information from the corps."

"Well, go on then, tell me what it is already?" Why is he being so slow delivering the information? "Did they catch the killer at last?"

"I wish. No, the thing is - two people have gone missing."

"Missing?" I am apprehensive, sure, but this sounds better than bodies being found once again.

"Oliwia knows them. Do the names Saskia and Fabrizio ring a bell to you?"

"I'm not sure they do." This can't be happening again. She looks so peaceful in front of me. I have to protect her, at all costs.

"Saskia was in the movie club with Oliwia."

"Oh, right. I've never met that group. I've heard about my daughter, Karla and some of the others at Europea attending of course, but I don't believe they mentioned any of their names. Who's Fabrizio?"

"A guard at the halls. He worked there when Oliwia still went to Europea Halls, so she must know him - at least a little."

"One of the guards? What happened, Lukas?"

"Him and Saskia were seen on the cameras on the grounds of Europea Halls, but once they entered the building, the footage was cut off."

"So someone must've tampered with the cameras?"

"Very likely."

"What does this mean? Do you think they're - gone?"

"All of this happened earlier today, so let's not panic just yet. But you deserve to know any information that is given to me."

"I appreciate that." I grab onto his arm, briefly. "Thank you. What now?"

"The entire team is on it and the moment I get any updates you'll be the first to know. Do you think we should tell Oliwia?"

"No!" I yell out instinctively. Mirek and Oliwia glance at us in confusion. I put on a fake smile and pretend I almost tripped. That was close. "No." I repeat quietly this time. "Absolutely not. Did you see her just now? She almost had a moment of actual happiness. We can't take that away from her until we know with certainty what has happened."

"I agree with you. Let's go back to the house. I'll keep you posted."

I remain silent for the rest of the walk back up to the mountain. The wind hits more violently as we climb up to the villa, as though warning me of what is yet to come.

Chapter 7

OLIWIA

I crack my back and neck – that damned tension hasn't left my body in years – and glare out of the large window from my bedroom as I wrap myself under my cosy blankets. The book I was trying to read wasn't registering; it's too hard to focus these days. The classes completely take it out of me, after that my energy for the day is usually gone.

A tiny boat at the edge of the horizon peacefully floats past. The ferry.

Red and white.

I swallow hard and push the past back. Don't push *her* back though, Liv. Karla. I force myself out of the visual and guide it to another memory.

Ingvild, Karla and I are sitting in bed in Budapest, staring out at the Danube. We're having breakfast together. There, that's better. I pretend the sea in front of me is the Danube and that my girls are sitting next to me. This feels safe. That was the only moment on our trip when we were actually safe. The only moment Karel wasn't around. He was on his jog at that time, or whatever the hell he was doing. Don't go there, he doesn't deserve your energy. I try to bring my focus back to Ingvild and Karla, but the red splotches on the white ferry force their way back into my brain. *Not now. Don't freeze.*

I spring out of bed and grab my mobile. *Keep moving. Don't freeze.* Just call him, he gets it. My heartbeat and sweaty hand palms are warning me. The alarm bell is going off in my head. I won't let it though, I know better by now. Remember Vera's words. Be kind to yourself, talk to your subconscious with understanding. We're okay guys, this is just a false alarm. You can relax. I speak to my subconscious as though they're a team of little helpers, all doing their best to keep me alive. Don't get aggravated, this is a natural reaction to trauma. Why can't I just relax?

"Liv?"

"Balazs! Hi, I -"

"Are you having an attack?" His voice is full of concern. Instant guilt, great, on top of everything else.

"I'm not sure. It's coming up. I'm sorry, I shouldn't have called you."

"I can hear it in your voice. Never apologise for reaching out. Stay with me. We can do the breathing trick together. I'm here, yeah?"

A hint of hope. "Yeah. You're here."

"We'll breathe in to the count of three and exhale to the count of five. I'll count and you follow my voice."

I mellow into the numbers. I'm a bit light-headed, but that always happens when my breathing has become shallow 'cause of the anxiety. Rationalise it. I'm not getting enough oxygen, that's why. My vision will become better. It always does. The brain fog will vanish. It always does, too. Balazs has the most soothing presence. His voice instantly calms me down.

CHAPTER 7

"Better?"

I exhale slowly again. "Much better. Thanks so much, Balazs."

"We promised we'd be there for each other. I don't believe in empty promises."

"Agreed."

"I'm sorry you've had to go through that again. At least it wasn't a full on attack. They seem to be getting lighter and less frequent?"

I hadn't noticed, but he's right. A small smile lifts me out of my sullen mood. "I guess so. You always know what to say. My mum starts freaking out when I panic, so I appreciate you staying so calm when I'm like this."

I hear a small cackle from the other end of the line. "She's drama personified, isn't she?"

"Ha, she sure is."

"But you know she means well."

"She does. They both do."

"Your dad is quite the serene guy from what you've told me, does he help in those moments?"

"He does, but I do hate to see his eyes fill with sadness when it happens. Sometimes he starts crying. It's probably hard for him to see his little girl like that. You're the only one I feel like really gets it."

"I do. Well, I try to. I definitely understand trauma better now." A heavy silence hangs in the air. I stare out at the sea in front of me, the moon now brightly reflected in the smooth waves. The chaos from the waves has settled. So have I. "Anyway, Liv, give me some updates. Lukas still doing your head in?"

"You bet, boo. It's almost as if he wants to become buddies

with me, which is a bit off-putting. He's always so damn smiley. My dad likes him though."

"He does?"

"Yeah, those two are always chattering in my dad's office. Can you imagine, *my* dad speaking in full sentences."

"Mirek, the beacon of silence, chattering? Seems hard to believe." Another small laugh. Even his laugh sounds warm and calm. I'm so glad I still have him in my life, even if it's virtual for now. Balazs had suggested moving to Spain with me, but I wasn't having any of that. Anyone who hangs around with me for too long - well, let's say I have the Sidney-Prescott-effect on my friends. I didn't want to put him in any more danger.

"I know, right? My mum still looks shocked when she hears how chatty he is around Lukas. I think she fancies him a bit, you know? Lukas, I mean."

"Well, you did say he's attractive."

"He is - a bit rugged with stubble and blonde, wavy hair. He's tall too. I can see the appeal. My mum would never act on anything though. Besides, I'm pretty sure he's gay."

"Really? You haven't told me that!"

"My gaydar goes off whenever I see his body language."

"So, maybe he's into your dad?"

"Balazs! That is the grossest thing I have ever heard! Do you want me to spew my soul out?"

More laughing, from both of us this time around. "It's funny though, you attract the queers, Liv."

"Ha, I know, boo." Tanya's gorgeous locks pop back into my mind. "Speaking of queers, I saw Tanya again today."

"Oooh." A teasing sound that makes me instantly regret I told him. "Do elaborate."

CHAPTER 7

"Don't! Anyway, she came over to the beach for a bit and asked me to go watch a movie at her place tomorrow night."

"Wait, wait, like an actual date without Lukas around?"

"Not a date, just a chill –"

"Call it whatever you want, but you're not supervised? How did your parents even agree to that?"

"Tanya has guards at her place, too."

"Of course she does. You rich people." Another tease.

"Hey, don't be like that! You're normally not the judgy type."

"Fine, fine, I take it back. Anyhow, cute that you're going to hers tomorrow. How are you feeling about it?"

"Guilty as can be. Like I'm cheating on Karla."

"I knew you'd say that. Completely understandable."

"So, you agree it's a bad idea?"

"What? I didn't say that! No, I think it's a great idea! You deserve to be around people your own age. You'll end up an old spinster with eighty-two rescue cats."

"That's an oddly specific number. At least they're rescues. Sounds great to me!"

"You know what I mean. It's just a movie."

"Is it? I think she's into me. I'm not sure, that sounds so arrogant."

"It doesn't, you're a great catch."

"A trauma-filled box, amazing catch."

"Don't talk about yourself that way Liv, you deserve happiness in your life. After everything that has happened, you're still good to the people around you."

"Those that are left. I know, I know. I'm being annoying. Anyway, I guess you're right. She *is* nice."

"And beautiful?"

I sigh. "Yes, beautiful too. But I'm not over Karla. I don't want to be."

"Then keep it amicable. Be clear with her that you're not ready. No reason why you can't be friends."

"Balazs, the voice of reason."

"For others, sure."

"Enough about me, how is it going in Budapest?" Poor guy, I shouldn't be that heavy around him all the time; he's lost Szofi.

"It's - going."

"Have you met anyone interesting?"

"Me? No, not at all. I'm not sure if relationships will ever be for me."

"That is absolutely fine. Has your aunt digested the news a bit by now?"

"Surprisingly, yes. She didn't quite get it at first, like I told you last time. It's funny, when I talked about you, she asked if you're also like me."

"Aroace?"

"Yes, she thinks that I only hang out with aroace people."

"Does she know I'm lesbian?"

"She does, she said it's nice that we have found each other. So, I suppose it shows you can't judge people. I was so dead set on her never accepting me fully, but look at her now."

"We're lucky in that sense, you and I. Having supportive families."

"Totally! Not everyone has that luxury in life. I'm really grateful my mum and Auntie are there for me. Never thought they'd move to Budapest, but we've built quite a nice home together."

"And overlooking the Parliament! The photos you sent me look stunning."

"Yeah, it's nice here. It's not the same without *her*, of

course."

My heart bleeds for him. I respect him so much for plowing through life and staying in Budapest. "I get that. Szofi would be so proud of you, Mr. Almost-Official-Psychologist!"

"It hasn't been easy, in all honesty. Some of the stuff I've been studying is very confronting, to say the least."

"The trauma course?"

"Yup. But it has given me something to hold onto. I understand myself better thanks to it. I understand *you* more as well."

"Ah yes, good ol' PTSD. Have you done your big presentation yet?"

"No, it's in two days. I'm all good to go. Saved everything on the Cloud, my PowerPoint is ready to kick ass."

"Good on you, man, you've got this. One last step before graduation. I'm so excited for you!"

"Thanks, Liv. I -" Balazs' mum is shouting something in the background. "I'll have to get going. Dinner's ready."

"Goulash?"

"No, pasta. Hungarians don't eat goulash every day, you know, Miss Pierogi."

We both chortle. "I'm actually having pierogi tonight. Tanya is making tapas for me tomorrow though. Anyway, go enjoy your pasta. Call me after your presentation, deal?"

"Deal. Love you, Liv."

"Love you too, boo."

Chapter 8

LUKAS

The seagull calls pull me back to the view in front of me. The Mediterranean is still at this time of day. Just a couple of small boats ever so gently rock the waves. I'm sitting in the ginormous living room and still can't quite believe how I ended up being selected for the job. I thought Jan would've made a far more logical choice, seeing as he worked so closely with LeBeaux, but Oliwia made it very clear she didn't trust anyone who worked directly under her. Still, I didn't expect to be the one chosen and I'm not sure how I feel about it all of these weeks later.

At first it seemed exciting, protecting an aristocratic family. When I was given the news that we'd move to the south of Spain to live in a secluded villa, I wasn't exactly weeping with sorrow. However, that secluded part is starting to weigh on me. These people are not my friends nor should they be. I'm here to do my job, meaning I have literally zero social life. Being uprooted like that is way more difficult than I thought it would be. All I can hope for is that my team at the corps finds the killer asap, so we can all move back home. This place could never feel like home. It feels like one of those places used in music videos to show modern wealth. I mean, in my opinion, the minimalism works

CHAPTER 8

for this type of house, but Basia's reaction made me laugh so much. I tried not to show it, but when she entered the place for the first time, she turned up the posh-dial with her forced British-ish English and yelped: "Oh how utterly devoid of any style or class, darlings! Where's the chandeliers? Where's the marble columns? It's all so painfully bare! Scandi chique never should've made it to the deep European south!" It even made Oliwia snicker. Part of this experience has felt a bit like a social experiment studying how the wealthy live. Basia seemed to be in mourning for her staff at first and Mirek complained he couldn't find the right type of cigars in town. The only actual chill one is the one who's gone through the unthinkable. Fine, she's not exactly warming up to me, but can you blame her? I wouldn't trust anyone around me after those murders, no way. With the killer still on the loose, I am surprised she is doing as well as she seemingly is. I notice the heaviness in her cadence when she talks about her friends and girlfriend, but she is still powering through somehow. I respect her a lot for that.

What has it been now? Five odd months? It appears like we have all more or less found a balance in this surrealistically odd situation. Basia and I often discuss art, Oliwia continues throwing me shade and Mirek and I have become close. Not exactly friends, I need to make sure I keep my distance, but he's such a good conversationalist, which you wouldn't think if you see him in group settings. Basia and Oliwia often joke that he is a one-liner kind of guy, but when it's just him and me the conversation never runs stale. He's a charming man as well. Those deep grey eyes pierce right through me when he is in one of his deep chat modes. I think he's happy he found someone else who's interested in politics. His eyes lit up with hope when Oliwia started taking EU law classes, but I'm not too convinced she's doing that solely out of interest in the actual subject. When Mirek realised Oliwia wasn't that into it, the deflated father found solace in me. The one thing we all *do* have in common is that we all appreciate art. We've spent some of our evenings together browsing through art catalogs and watching documentaries about Spanish art history. We're not supposed to peruse the area around us too much, so we're learning about it through TV.

"Hey Lukas." Mirek looks at me with a warm, inviting smile.

I hadn't expected him just yet. "Hey Mirek."

"I have an extra glass of port wine in my office if you'd care to join me?"

"Absolutely."

Chapter 9

TANYA

My mum closes the door behind her and gives me a little wave before leaving our home. I'm grateful she is a bit more aware of social conduct than Oliwia's parents and gives me some space for tonight. I exhale slowly and have a look around the main hall. It's filled with all types of succulents and paintings of our family. I wonder what she'll think when she walks in. I know she is well off too, but this style might not be her thing at all. Belgian villas are quite different from Spanish ones. It might all look a bit tacky to her. So what? Why would that even matter? It's so hard to read her that everything makes me nervous. I hope I did everything right. I set up the cinema room, "The Babadook" is ready. I was a bit surprised at her choice, didn't think she'd go for horror, but I can imagine it was a conscious decision on her part. Not sure why, but I'll roll with it. I love a good horror flick. Lukas better not be playing a prank on me. How awkward would it be if I start playing a horror film when that's the last thing she wants to watch? I need to double check with her if that is really what she asked for. Girl, chill, for real. Right, Tinto de Verano. I need me a good drink. I want to call for our in-house chef, but realise he has likely gone home by now. At least he prepared some lovely tapas for movie night before heading off. I guess it'd be rude to ask the guards if they can fix me a drink. Whatever, I'll just do it myself.

Suddenly, there's a knock on the door. Mum probably forgot her keys again, nothing new there. I walk past the cacti towards the main door and open up. No one. I peer around the driveway, the porch lights illuminating the path in front of the door. The trimmed bushes around the graveled path look pristine, as always.

"Mum?"

No reply. Perhaps Oliwia arrived early. I thought Lukas would send me a text when they're on their way. This is odd.

"Liv?"

Not a single sound outside, except for the distant seagull calls. Weird. I grab my mobile and call my mum. She picks up straight away. I keep looking outside, in case I see any movement.

"Is she there yet? Are you two having fun?"

"Mum, Christ, relax. No, she hasn't arrived yet. Did you knock on the door a second ago?"

"Knock on the -? What? I'm in the car, Tanya."

"Oh, right." Still nobody around. The sea breeze causes the bushes to dance in an eerily elegant fashion against the black sky.

"Tan, are you okay?"

"I - I think so, I definitely heard knocking, but there's nobody here."

"Get the guards, now!" The panic in her voice kicks me into action. "And lock the doors!"

I shut the door tight, activate the central alarm system and make a run for it, towards the guards' quarters at the end of the hallway. I swing the door open and see the three guards playing cards, confusion filling their wide eyes.

"Are they there?" Mum asks.

I'm a bit out of breath, so I take a moment to reply.

"Well?"

"Yes, they're here, Mum. Don't worry, probably just my imagination."

A guard named Emanuel stands up and walks towards me, putting one hand on the gun in his back pocket. "Is everything alright, Miss Tanya?"

"I think so. I heard knocking on the front door, but there was nobody there."

He looks at me sternly and grabs my arm. "Stay here, Miss, I'll go check."

I nod. I am probably exaggerating. Dani and Javi set down their deck of cards and signal me to sit down with them.

"Tan, what's happening over there?"

"It's okay, Mum, I'm with the guards. I think I'm a bit tense because of Oliwia coming over. I'm so sorry for bothering you."

"Don't ever worry about that, sweetheart! You're okay then?"

"I'm - I'm fine. I'm with Dani and Javi."

"Good, stay there until Oliwia arrives."

"Okay, Mum. Enjoy your night out with dad, talk to you tomorrow."

"Are you sure? I can stay on the line until Manu is back."

"No, honestly, this is silly. I shouldn't have called. These prank calls happen all the time at our place."

"If anything is up, doesn't matter what, you can call me, I'll be over in less than fifteen minutes."

"Fine, Mum, thanks. Bye now."

"Bye love."

We all sit silently at the table. I'm not sure why but it's taking Emanuel so long to come back.

"Should we check on Manu?"

Javi instantly replies. "Let's give him a moment. It's better for you to stay here with us, Miss Tanya."

"Okay, if you say so. He'll be fine, won't he?"

"Absolutely, he knows what he's doing."

The minutes tick by, dauntingly slow. I scan the guards' quarters and focus my stare on the window, looking for any sign of an intruder outside. Still nothing.

Pling. Text message from an unknown number.

I jump up and scream.

"What is it, Miss?" Dani stands up and looks ready for battle.

"Sorry, I got a text message. I was startled." I need to get it together, what kind of a date will it be tonight if I'm a bundle of nerves? That's the last thing Oliwia needs. I check the message.

Unknown Number: *We're on our way. We'll be there in about twenty.*

Oh, right, I forgot to save Lukas' number. That calms me down a little. Where the heck is Manu though?

The door bursts open, it's him. I jolt up again. He inhales sharply through his nose, his mouth tense and pursed.

"What is it, Emanuel?"

"We're fine, Miss. There was someone on the premises, but I scared him away."

"Excuse me? Somebody on the grounds *here*? What did he want?"

CHAPTER 9

"I'm not sure, I only saw a black-hooded man racing past, he was probably looking to break in. I couldn't make out a face, it was too dark out there. But I assure you, Miss, he won't be coming in. Not on our watch. I showed him the gun and told him to stay away."

"Should we call the police?"

"That won't be necessary, we'll make sure we stay extra vigilant tonight."

"Okay, thanks." I'm not entirely convinced, but I know these guys take their job very seriously - when they're not playing cards - and this happens at least once a month, annoyingly. "Can you all do me a favour, please?" I look at all three of them.

"Anything, Miss." Javi answers.

"Could we not mention this to Oliwia please? She has been through some things and I don't want her to worry over nothing. Keep your eyes and ears open, but don't look menacing or anything. I beg you. I want tonight to go well."

They all smile and nod in agreement. My face feels hot with anxiety. I need to freshen up before Liv arrives, I probably look an absolute state right now. Shake it off, it's not the first time someone tried to break in here. Most people in Murcia know who we are. Still, doesn't make it any less scary.

It's fine, tonight will be fun. Finally, some one-on-one time with Oliwia.

Chapter 10

OLIWIA

I swear, if Mum were given the chance, she'd have taken a photo of me - prom style - before heading off with Lukas. She was beaming with pride. Looks like she's more excited about tonight than I am. I faked a bit of excitement, cause it was genuinely nice seeing her being so positive. Luckily, Lukas ushered me into the limousine before she had the chance for a photo shoot. Don't get me wrong, I appreciate that she cares, but the woman can be so damn pushy.

The left back tyre of the limo bumps into the rough street. Lukas looks stressed out. To be fair, these winding mountain roads were not designed for limos. Nor is Lukas a professional driver.

"So sorry Oliwia, not the easiest of roads here." He whispers apologetically.

"It's fine." I hesitate whether I should talk a bit more, cause Balazs did make me ponder about something after our call. He mentioned I'm kind to the people around me, but nothing could be further from the truth when it comes to Lukas. Perhaps it wouldn't hurt to show some friendliness to him. Doesn't mean I need to fully trust him. "You're doing well."

He looks completely shocked, and that right there says it all,

CHAPTER 10

I must've been so horrible to him so far. He continues down the road and doesn't reply.

"I'm sorry Lukas. I know I haven't been the nicest to you."

He looks back at me in the rearview mirror. "I get it."

"Seriously. You've been so patient with me, you must think I'm an absolute bitch."

He chuckles. "Not quite. I don't think you trust me and frankly, I don't blame you." That comment takes me aback. I wonder if I should reply honestly to that or play nice. "You don't have to reply to that, Oliwia. I was thinking about this yesterday actually. I don't think I'd be able to trust people around me after everything."

I look outside the backseat window and spot the palm trees lining the coastline beneath me. They're lit up by the street lights that follow the small promenade. Soon we'll be turning inland to the capital city of Murcia. "I - I don't know what to say to that."

"No need for a reply. Sorry if I'm being too direct."

"No, not at all. Like I said, you've been so respectful. I have a hard time trusting people, true. I'd like to trust you. But whenever I lower my walls, someone takes advantage of me. Who says you're different?"

He takes a while to answer. I don't see any signs of him being offended though, he might be weighing his words carefully.

"I can't convince you on that one. I believe your instincts must be strong by now. You can most likely gauge people quite well."

"I'd like to think so. But you know. Lucija, Karel. I did trust them wholeheartedly."

I hope I don't regret this later on, but it is so emotionally and physically exhausting not trusting anyone. Sometimes it is easier to let my guard down, as contradicting as that may sound. It's scary too, won't lie. This better not bite me in the ass later. Tread carefully.

"So talking about trusting people, let me put my cop nose on. What do you know about this girl Tanya?"

"Why are you asking?"

"Because you're about to walk into someone's house. Someone you don't really know very well. I want you to be prepared."

He's right. Somehow I've been so nervous about going over I hadn't even thought about this potentially being dangerous. He throws me a quick look. "Is it okay that I am asking this?"

"It is. I'm a bit thrown off by that question, but it's a good one. Let's see. I've only met her like five times. I know she's into films a lot, like me. She's wealthy."

"Like you." He winks at me.

"I suppose so. She's third generation, Kenyan descent. She cares a lot about her roots, which I think is really important. She's close to her parents."

"That's a good sign."

"I'd like to think so. Also, she graduated with honours in Art history, so we have our love for arts in common."

"And what kind of person is she?"

"Tough to say. She acts a bit nervous around me, so I'm not entirely sure I've seen the real Tanya yet."

"I think I know why she's nervous." He says playfully.

"Please don't make this a big deal, like my mum does."

"I'll play it cool, like your dad."

He's right, Dad has been more relaxed about the entire non-date thing. But then again, he's rarely stressed out. I notice we're entering the city now, we're not too far from the old town. The glimmering street lights are reflected in the river Segura.

CHAPTER 10

Once we cross the bridge, we'll be in Tanya's area. Bridge. The Chain Bridge. Not now, stay present.

"Good, thanks. I think she's kind, she cares about how I feel and wants to make me feel comfortable. So much so that it makes me a bit -"

"Uncomfortable?"

"Exactly. It's so obvious people often don't know how to act around me, like I'm this fragile wounded bird that needs healing, which they think they can provide somehow."

"That must be tiring."

"So bloody tiring!" I'm surprised at how understanding he is. I need to give him some credit for reading me so spot on. Either that or he's been studying me to get me at my weakest moment. I decide that I'm undecided on Lukas. When we get back I'll ask him more about *his* life. Partly out of interest, partly out of self-protection.

"Tanya's estate is a couple of blocks away. Have a good time tonight and know that you can always reach me if something feels fishy. I'll be parking my car down the road and staying close by, just in case."

"But then my parents don't have any protection." A touch of anxiety creeps in. The killers have never killed any older relatives, why would they now? Balazs did say the killer had taken a photo of his mum and aunt, but they were never harmed. Let's go with older people not being the demographic, bar the old lady on the bridge and Arpad. That poor innocent man, trying to help us out. I still remember the way he wobbled over to the front door in his slippers. Shake it off, Liv, if the killer wanted my parents dead, he could've done it ages ago.

"Would you like me to go back to your parents?"

"Better safe than sorry, right? There are guards at Tanya's

house."

"Fair enough. I'll drop you off and make sure the guards are home first, if you are good with that."

"Great." I pause for a moment, thinking about this entire conversation, a sense of gratitude warming my chest. "Thank you for the talk, Lukas. I won't treat you so poorly in the future. Unless you're a masked maniac. The jury's out on that one."

He smiles again. "That's a fair call." We drive up the graveled road towards Tanya's massive estate. "Enjoy yourself tonight."

The moment one of the guards opens the main doors, I look back at Lukas who signals an "okay" sign, heading back to the limo.

"Welcome, Miss Oliwia. My name is Javier. Miss Tanya is waiting for you in the cinema room." That is a bit formal, but then again, I'm not too sure about how these things work in aristocratic circles in Spain. It's all a bit more loose in Belgium. The guard looks kind enough, but more importantly - built like a bulldozer and with a gun in his back pocket. He reminds me of the Arms at Europa Halls. They didn't end up protecting me, but I'll take what I can get.

"Thank you, Javier."

"If you'd be so gracious as to follow me, I will guide you to the cinema."

"Why, thank you." Why am I turning into my mum? Whenever I'm unsure in a posh social situation, I end up sounding like a constipated royal.

I put my Ingvild-goggles on and peer around the villa. I'm not sure if she would've liked this style as much as the Art Nouveau townhouses back home - wherever home is nowadays - but it is definitely a sight to behold. Besides the copious amount

CHAPTER 10

of plants everywhere, I notice the minimal embellishments and smooth stucco around me. The sandstone elements add to the Mediterranean feel of the house. The ceilings aren't as high as I'm used to, but the white arches that lead up to the marble staircase do give it an air of grandiosity - only more austere looking than the Belgian villas.

Javier leads me up the stairs to the first floor, and I study the family portraits. They're omnipresent. Paintings in what I'd call Realist style (don't kick me if I'm wrong, Ingvild) show the entire lineage, dating back many generations. This is not new money, that's for sure.

We continue onto the first floor where there are even more plants and portraits, alongside some terracotta vases and futuristic sculptures adorning the hallway. I've never taken in details as much before. That's one of the many things I loved about Ingvild. She'd tell me all about these intricate little details on the facades of Brussels' houses built on small cobble streets. At the time, I did listen, but it didn't really sink in. Now I take in every possible detail. For her. The colour palette in the hall is mostly warm yellow hues with touches of earth tones and muted reds, a very harmonious and calming effect on the eyes. Nothing necessarily extravagant, but classy in an understated way.

"Liv, you've made it!" Tanya is standing by the door, two glasses in hand. She looks as nervous as I feel, so at least I'm not alone in this.

"I did, this place is gorgeous!"

"Really? I mean, I'm glad you like it!"

"Absolutely, all these earthy tones." I either sound like a connoisseur or an obnoxious twat right now.

"That's mostly my dad's input, believe it or not. My mum

doesn't really care about the interior. As long as we live secluded, with enough space to entertain, she's happy." Too much rich talk, let's switch it up.

"So, movie night!" Not too sure why I keep shouting instead of talking like a normal human being, but she's doing the same. Nervous energy?

"Exactly, here, take this." I walk up to her, give her a soft kiss on the cheek, and take the wine glass. "I prepped us a little Tinto de Verano."

"What's in that again?"

"It's basically red wine with lemonade. A staple in summer in the south of Spain. I know it's winter, but why the heck deny ourselves the pleasures of summer?"

Sounds disgustingly enticing. I'm down. "Thanks."

She guides me into the cinema room, which is enormous. It is the size of an actual cinema, I thought it'd be some fancy room with some plush chairs and a projector, but there are about a hundred seats in here. Old-school red velvet chairs with a larger than life screen.

"What do you think?" She smiles, eager for confirmation.

"This is amazing. What the actual?" I gawk around the room and can't believe what I'm seeing. There's more embellishments here for sure. Golden columns on the edges of the room, the ceiling is covered in what I suppose are Kenyan motives. I could happily live here. "Can I move in?"

Tanya giggles and turns red. Crap, that didn't come out the way I wanted to. Don't lead her on tonight.

"Of course you can, you're always welcome here." She takes my hand and walks me up to the back row. "Is here okay? I always love sitting up here, overlooking the entire room." Either that, or she's thinking of the classic make out spot in

CHAPTER 10

cinemas.

"Cheers!" She clinks her glass against mine and we both take a big gulp. My lips have dried up since I've arrived and I'm thirstier than I realised. I can't think of anything to say.

"So, "The Babadook"? That is what you wanted to watch, right? Lukas texted me, so I wanted to check with you if-"

"Yes, yes, that's what I told Lukas."

"Oh, great. Pleasantly surprised. So, you like your horror?"

"Elevated horror. I didn't for a while, but I do like watching it, yes."

"Is that what it's called? Sounds posh." She winks at me and vehemently pokes me in the ribs, to which I cry out in pain. She looks mortified.

"Oh, god, I'm so sorry! Sometimes I don't know my own strength."

I gently rub my ribs, not wanting to make a big deal out of it. "It's fine, no worries." This is becoming more awkward by the minute, perhaps I should leave. That'd be rude though, she's set this entire thing up. Think of something to say, come on. Horror, right.

"Yes, it's called elevated horror, cause it's not just about the jump scares and the killing."

"Like slashers?"

Great, the word I was trying to avoid. "Yes. Like slashers."

"I see, what are some other ones in the genre then?"

"Let's see. "The Witch" is a good one, then there's "Midsommar" or "Get Out" for example."

"All those are considered elevated horror? I had no idea. I can see why, now you mention it. They're all excellent films. It pisses me off that horror is often so overlooked and looked down on."

Okay, now we're getting in the flow. "Right? There are so many good actors, directors, screenwriters - you name it - out there that won't ever get an Oscar nomination, just cause the film is labelled horror."

"Ridiculous. That's like Jamie Lee Curtis playing Laurie Strode in, how many "Halloween" films?"

"Seven I think, if you count "Halloween Resurrection", which -"

"Which we won't." We both laugh. "The point is, she recently got an Oscar, but of course it wasn't for her Final Girl role. So dumb." I like this geeky side to her, not many girls would know this stuff. There could be potential here, for a friendship I mean. Only that, I'm not ready for more.

"Agreed. Or Kevin Williamson, my all time favourite screenwriter."

"Oh, he wrote "Scream", didn't he?"

"Yes, but he worked on so many other classics like "I Know What You Did Last Summer", "The Faculty", "Halloween H20"."

"Wow okay, all the 90s classics basically."

"Yes, and he recently released "Sick" and worked on the new "Scream" flicks too, but I haven't watched those ones yet." The truth is, I can't stomach watching slashers anymore after - you know. One day I might be ready, but there are too many triggers.

Tanya is staring me deep in the eyes. "You're so knowledgeable about film. I love that about you."

I lower my eyes and glare at my drink. I think I'm blushing.

"Thanks."

She glides her index finger underneath my chin and gently pushes up my face. We're looking into each other's eyes now.

CHAPTER 10

She's so stunning, I can't deny it. Those full lips and warm, inviting eyes. She's leaning in for - Oh, no way, she's leaning in for a kiss. *Abort mission, abort mission.* I push back.

"I can't, sorry, I can't yet. I'm still in love with Karla."

Tanya flops herself down in the seat next to me, completely deflated. "I am such a fool."

"No, you're not! You're gorgeous and loving and geeky, I like all those things about you. I'm just not - there."

"I can't believe I went there. I'm genuinely so sorry."

"It's fine." We sit in silence for what feels like an eternity. "Perhaps I should leave though."

She looks at me again, deep hurt settled in her eyes. "Really? But I was about to bring in the tapas and we haven't even watched the film yet."

"I know, but I-"

"Please stay, just as friends, Liv." This time, hearing my nickname triggers something deep inside me. She is not supposed to say my name like that. I never told her to. Some sort of anger and frustration grows inside me, wanting a release. I have to leave, now.

I jump up and run out of the room. Tanya shouts at me as I close the door behind me: "Wait!" But I can't. The name Liv was for the Europea Halls group. The name that was taken away from me when all of my friends from Brussels were taken away from me. The only reason I allow Balazs to call me that is because he knows, he gets it, he's been through it too. Tanya doesn't know me, not like that.

I storm down the main hall and ask Javier to open the doors. He does so, looking highly confused. It reminds me of those cops that were guarding our doors at the halls when Ingvild, Lucija - that bitch - and I were fighting in front of them. Grown ass men who have no idea how to behave around an angry woman.

I stand out there, next to the road, mentally blocking the estate behind me. I cry out a guttural pain that had been festering for far too long. The tears roll down, gushing down as if I only have this one shot in life to cry. *I'm so sorry, Karla, I shouldn't have even considered going out yet. Please forgive me.* The tears keep coming, my abdomen hurting from the hard sobs being released. This pain is blinding, I don't want to feel it anymore, but I know I have to allow it. My entire body is exhausted, crippled by pain and trauma release. It's like the deepest teenage heartbreak, times infinity. It pulls the air out of my lungs. The deepest, rawest version of pain. Who have I been kidding this entire time, I'm not okay. Nowhere near it. I don't know how to ever build up a friendship or relationship again, ever.

The bushes next to me rustle loudly. I snap out of it.

I scan the bushes, darkened with the edges faintly shimmering from the porch lights in the distance. I heard something. I definitely did. I'm smart enough to not ask who's there, but I'm too scared to move.

A dark hooded figure steps out from behind the bush in front of me. I can't make out a face, nor do I need to. I scream and spring towards the main road. I grab a hold of my phone and ring Lukas whilst running. *Don't look back, keep going. You know how this works.* I hear footsteps behind me, he's following me. Pick up, Lukas, damn it, pick up.

The limo is parked at the end of the road. Why is it there? He's supposed to be at the villa. I continue down the road, the heavy footsteps sounding closer. Then they stop. No more

CHAPTER 10

sounds behind me. I turn around and look at the blackened road. The street, the bushes in the distance, the seagulls flying over the city, but no figure. Nowhere.

A hand grabs my shoulder. I yelp and am ready to swing- it's Lukas.

"Oliwia! What's wrong?"

"Where the hell have you been? Why didn't you answer my call?"

"I saw you running down the street. What happened?"

"He's here. The killer - he's here."

I take a step back and scan his posture. No hood, but the rest of his stance resembles the figure too much for it to be a coincidence. "*You*. I knew it."

"Ho, wait, hold on! I didn't do anything."

"Then why on earth are you still here? Step back!"

"Alright, okay, calm down."

"Don't you tell me to calm down! Why are you not at home?"

"I - I wanted to wait a bit, to make sure you were okay."

"I told you there were guards around."

"I know, but it's my job to protect you."

"Get the hell away from me!" I step back even further and try to catch my breath. The hair on my arms stands on end. Stay alert here.

I'm pushed down to the ground. What's happening? Is Lukas attacking me?

"You, come back here!" Lukas is shouting out. I look back up and notice the dark hooded figure running away from us. "I have a gun, stand still or I'll shoot!"

"Shoot him!" I yell back.

Gun shots are released in the air, flying away into the darkness of the evening. He's out of sight.

"Oliwia, get in the car!"

"But what if he's –"

"Now!" A mean, deep growl shows me Lukas means business.

I rush inside the limo and lock the doors. Lukas runs off into the poorly lit road, I can just about make out where he is. *Be careful.* I take hold of my phone again and text Tanya. If Mum knew I secretly jotted down her number, she'd be mad. Or happy?

Oliwia: *This is Liv's number. Man in a hood running away, be careful. Alert guards!*

I ball my hands into fists and rock back and forth, steadying myself. *Don't lose it, stay here.* I take out the pocket knife, which I should've done ages ago, but I was too frozen to think clearly. Okay, think. What did you see? A person wearing a black hoodie, but I'm not sure I saw a mask. What if it's someone else? That's probably naive of me. It must be the killer. If for once I can count on someone to do their job, Lukas could take him out – right here, right now. This can all be over. Third act, done, in the blink of an eye. That thought gives me a glimmer of hope. I don't see Lukas anymore. Perhaps they're fighting. No gun shots either, I surely would've heard that. A flash of Ayat rushes past me, sitting in her limo during the last minutes of her life. Not now, I'm sorry Ayat, but I need to stay here.

Then I spot Lukas, gun still in hand, tense as can be. He holds up a flashlight in one hand, carrying the gun with the other. This isn't good. He's walking back to the limo and jumps in.

"So?"

"Nothing, I couldn't find anyone. We need to go home *now.*"

CHAPTER 10

He turns on the engine and sets the vehicle in motion.

"And then what?"

"We need to assess the situation with your parents and I will call the corps."

"Meaning?"

"Meaning either we stay put in the villa, not moving, or head back to Brussels."

That sets off yet another panic button inside me. "Brussels? Why?"

"Because if this is the actual killer, that means he knows where you are and you'd be safer in Brussels, where there's an entire police team on high alert. Let's get home first." The tyres are screeching against the rocky pavement, rushing forth to the villa. "Keep an eye out if you see anyone suspicious, Oliwia."

"I - Okay, I will." My heart is pounding against my chest and I'm all too conscious of the symptoms that are about to break out. "Lukas, I'm sorry. I shouldn't have suspected you." He could still be an accomplice, but for now I need to trust him. I need him to get me home.

"I get it, just focus on what you can spot outside. He might still be out there."

Chapter 11

TANYA

I need a moment to gather my thoughts. I always do this. I go in too deep too soon. I should have learned my lesson by now and understand that it scares off women. This is all so deeply humiliating. I don't think I ever want to see her again, I couldn't face her.

I walk out to the hallway, where the three musketeers are eager for me to spill the tea.

"Don't." I say bluntly.

"What about the tapas?" Dani wonders.

"*That's* what you're worried about? Have them, they're in the kitchen."

"I mean, only if you –"

"For Christ's sake, have all the patatas bravas in the world, just give me some space. Shoo, shoo, all of you! By the way, Oliwia's texted me that she's also seen that creep wearing a hoodie. Make sure you check the grounds please." I wave them out of the hallway. They don't need much convincing. Let them handle the creep burglar, I've had it with tonight. That gives me time to sneak off into the casino to have some time to myself. My parents won't be back for some hours, so that gives me plenty of time to walk around the casino and centre myself. It's

CHAPTER 11

my happy space. I have a spare set of keys, so sometimes I go in at night when the house is locked. It's a museum during the day, but my playground at night. I basically grew up there.

I unlock the main gate and step into the dark entry hall of the casino. I lock it up behind me again to make sure no drunk tourists can get in, 'cause it was quite rowdy outside in the streets. As I switch on the lavish ornamental lights, the colourful Moorish tiles and golden ceilings welcome me, bathing me in comfort.

I continue down the hall into the large square atrium, full of Greek statues and golden chandeliers. I touch Aphrodite, which my mum would highly disapprove of, but I love touching these centuries-old statues. There's something about being one with history that soothes my mind, especially when it's racing the way it is now. I wanted to show Oliwia these rooms, but guess it's back to me, myself and I.

As I turn left, I spot the stands with medieval weaponry in the next room. Admittedly, this entire museum is a bit of a mishmash of styles, anachronistic at times, yet a fun labyrinth full of discoveries. I remember Dad telling me they're doing up this room, as the displays are becoming a bit dated. I didn't know they were already at it though, as I notice one of the glass display cases is empty. What's supposed to be in this one again? Ah yeah, that round ball thingy with the spikes. I read the sign underneath, marked "Morning Star". Bit of a euphemism for a heavy ball that can knock your brains out. For anyone who tells me I'm an oddball for liking horror, have a little gander at history, people. We've always been a messed up bunch.

The lights in the room go off. I look over my shoulder at

the light switches, but nobody's there. Another power cut, presumably. I walk towards the switches, but to no avail, it seems like I need to check the fuse box or the breaker box.

A slight shadow glides past the Greek statues in the back of the atrium. Somebody else is here. The thought of that hooded figure from before crosses my mind. What if he's followed me here? Who was Oliwia actually trying to warn me about? How did anyone even get in here, I locked up after I came in. A tightness forms around my throat, a barbed wire-like sensation pervading me. The figure is all the way at the back of the atrium, perhaps he hasn't noticed me. I squint my eyes, trying to make out where the shadow has gone.

I decide to head for the powder room next to the one I'm in and hide there. I swiftly walk towards the room and close the door behind me. There aren't any locks in here. Great. Alright, think, what would Laurie Strode do? The lights flicker on. I bite into my lower lip. *You've got this.*

A loud rumbling noise comes from behind the door. Crap, this can't be good. I grab my mobile to call the cops. Seven missed calls, all from the guards. I call back Javi's number, hoping they can make it here in time.

"Miss Tanya? Where are you?"

I whisper: "I can't talk loudly, I'm in the casino. I think someone followed me here." Another odd noise pops up from behind the door; it sounds like something has fallen onto the floor.

"Which room are you in?"

"The powder room. The one with all the golden mirrors. Hurry. Please."

"Stay put, we're coming over right away."

"Thank you, call the -"

CHAPTER 11

The door is smashed open. A cracked white mask glares at me. I scream as loud as I possibly can and smash the phone into the mask. I hear a distorted sound coming from my phone: "Miss, are you okay? What's happening? Guys, we need to leave!"

The figure takes my phone and smashes it to the ground. He is blocking the door, I have nowhere to run.

I bite down on my lower lip, figuring out what to do next. It doesn't look like he's carrying a weapon, just black gloves. *Fight.* I run into him and slam my fists against his chest, but I can tell there's some sort of armour underneath. He grabs my shoulders and pushes me deeper into the room. I shout for help and try to wriggle free, but his grip is too firm. His thumbs are pressing down deep onto my clavicle.

"Get off me! Let go!" He forces my body towards the golden mirrors. I've got to escape. There has to be a way out.

The figure grabs my locks, twists me around and pushes my entire body into the mirrors. I close my eyes and hear the glass being shattered into a million pieces. A sharp pain protrudes my skull. He pulls my head back, I open my eyes for a split second to orientate myself. My entire face is full of tiny glass shards, there's blood everywhere. I try to control my breathing. "Please, let me go!" He pushes my face back into the mirror. More pain, deeper cuts, blood dripping down my forehead and cheeks. Keep your eyes closed. Don't look now. Then a third blow into the mirror. A shard cuts through my left eye socket, partially blinding me. I can't pass out now. I push out of his grip and miraculously make it out this time. You still have your right eye, *run.*

I jolt past the weaponry room, with the killer a mere couple of steps behind me. I smash the door closed, but he's holding onto the frame, so I let go and continue on down the atrium.

I hear the rattling of chains, so I glance back to discover he is holding the morning star. A sense of angst overcomes me. *Don't stop now, keep going.*

The Greek goddesses stare at me with a hint of desperation in their eyes as I stride past them. The killer smashes the morning star into Aphrodite, the entire sculpture, and all its history, splinter into pieces, exploding in the atrium. My heart sinks as I see the remains lying on the ground. He is taunting me, showing off his power. He swings the heavy weapon in my direction, but I narrowly escape it.

I jump into the ballroom, the gorgeous grand piano and diamond chandeliers are a rough contrast with the horrors that lie behind. I glance around the room for a way out, but the spiral case up to the first floor mezzanine doesn't look like a smart move right now.

The deadly ball swooshes past me again, almost brushing my skin. I scream out and keep running down the ballroom, moving past the piano. I see the morning star being spun around again, inching towards my face.

My entire body crashes onto the grand piano, he's hit me. Everything goes black.

I gasp and inhale forcefully, as if coming above water after a long dive. The morning star is stuck inside the left side of my face. I try to move, but everything hurts too much. I'm lying on top of the piano's wing, which is echoing off key notes as if wailing for its life. The killer is standing in an ominous pose, ready for whatever is next in his morose plan. I can't see very well anymore, my eyesight turning blurry. Part of me wants to speak and protest by screaming, but I don't want him to see the pain I'm in. I'm not allowing him that pleasure. It's all I

CHAPTER 11

have left, my own act of rebellion.

The killer yanks off the morning star from my face and to my absolute horror I feel a part of my cheek being torn off. The fleshy red strings stick like glue to the weapon and some tiny pieces fly around the room, others landing back on the piano with a horrific moist splashy sound. Against my better judgment, I touch my cheek with my hands and notice I can feel the bones of my jaw. There is barely any skin left. This time I can't hold back the tears.

I roll off the piano and smack onto the ground, face down. Bits of flesh are hanging off my cheek as I see blotches of red spilling onto the floor. The killer remains in the same position, standing next to me, waiting on my next move. He steps onto my left hand, the bones cracking underneath his heavy boot. I cry out in agony. *Stand up, come on.* I hold onto the side of the piano as I lever the weight of my broken body upright. My neck muscles tired of the weight, I breathe heavy sighs. The figure steps closer and grabs me from the back, lifting me up. I want to protest, but my body won't cooperate. He starts off in the direction of the spiral staircase and drags me up. Step by step. I fall in and out of consciousness, not sure where I am anymore. *Do it already, kill me.* Up another step, I look down to the side of the stairs and notice the broken instrument covered in blood stains. My blood. The tears mixed with droplets of blood mix into a dark pink liquid spreading out onto the steps of the staircase, leading up high and higher.

We made it to the landing. On the left of me I see the bookcase filled with old books on Murcia's history. On the right I see the diamond chandelier, hanging metres above the piano. I can feel him breathing down my neck, his mask right behind me. Preceded by a loud grunt, he throws me into the light fixture.

With my last reflexes I hold onto the thick chain, resting my body on top of the diamond pearl drops of the chandelier. I look down, all too aware of the ceiling being over four metres tall. I can't hold my grip for long, I'm shocked I'm even managing this long. The killer fastens his grip around the morning star handle and swirls it at me. I close my eyes, but notice he hasn't hit me this time. He hit the chain though, so the entire chandelier is dancing around erratically. I clutch onto the chain for dear life. He takes a second go and hits the chain again. The moving intensifies and I feel my legs are slipping. It's over. I'm done fighting. I can't anymore.

"Just do it!" I let out with my last strength. The killer smashes the weapon into the chain a third time. I hear the cracking noise. This is it.

The chandelier, and me on top of it, falls down. As the wind caresses my cheeks one final time, I close my eyes and wait for the impact.

Chapter 12

BASIA

"Mirek, darling, they're here!"

He looks up from his book, barely with it. "What?"

"Liv and Lukas, the limo is pulling up to the driveway."

"Already? It's not even -" He checks his watch. "Ten o'clock. Bad date?"

"Presumably. Our poor darling. Do me a favour and be a tad bit more eloquent than your usual minimalist approach to consoling. She will need us."

He scoffs. "Fine."

Oliwia bursts into the door, face swollen with tears, as Lukas paces behind her.

"What on God's green earth has happened to you, my love?"

"The killer."

Both Mirek and I instantly stand up. He is holding on tight to that book of his. *Stay poised, Basia, your daughter needs you.*

"Care to elaborate?"

"Why are you talking in English?" She looks back at Lukas and nods. "Oh, I get it. Anyway, I saw someone wearing a dark hood tonight outside Tanya's home. He was hiding behind the bushes."

An invisible hand strangles my throat. "I see. Did you get the chance to have a look at the person's face?"

"No. I'm not sure if there was a mask or not. But the hoodie, the stance, the height. It felt like the same killer."

This is not the time to try and rationalise everything. Take your daughter seriously, she deserves it. "So what happened after you spotted them?"

Lukas takes over. "He pushed Oliwia to the ground. I ran after the figure, but couldn't find them. We drove straight back."

Mirek inches closer to our daughter and gives her a warm hug. That breaks her. Oliwia starts melting into his arms, tears running down. She was so close to having an enjoyable night and now this occurred. It is truly earth-shattering.

"Where was Tanya in all of this?" I wonder out loud.

"She - now don't freak out, promise?"

"Promise." I think I'm doing pretty great in all fairness.

"She tried to kiss me, but I panicked and ran off. That's when I spotted the figure. I texted her, I wanted to warn her."

"So she has your number now?" That throws me off a little. Nobody in Murcia is supposed to have her number.

"I had to, Mum, she needs to be careful."

"So, how is Tanya now?"

My darling looks rather rattled at the sound of that question. "I haven't called her yet. We were on our way back, looking out for the potential killer."

Lukas interjects. "Maybe it's a good idea to ring her now that we're all together."

She agrees and switches on her mobile.

Chapter 13

OLIWIA

The moment I am about to ring Tanya, Mum's phone goes off. We all jump a little, the entire room filled with anxiety-inducing electricity.

"Yes, hello? This is she." It doesn't sound like she knows the caller. My dad frowns at me; I'm lost too.

"Oh dear lord, I am ever so sorry. I shall - yes, absolutely. I will be in touch with you. Goodbye now." Her face contorted in heaviness, it sinks in. This is about Tanya. I clench my fists, fighting the invisible.

"Tell us, Mum. She's dead, isn't she?"

"I'm beyond sorry, my darling, but Tanya-"

"Is she dead or not, Mum?"

"Yes darling. She was found murdered in the royal casino. It was one of her guards who rang me."

The seagulls outside call out more frantically than they usually do, mocking my life. All the sounds are ringing sharply, the colours turning grey.

"Oliwia, stay with us." My dad takes my hand and squeezes it. He knows the symptoms by now. "We're here. Your mum and I are here for you and we're not leaving you behind."

"I-I'm here for you too." Lukas stumbles over his words.

"Would you be so kind as to get my daughter some ice cubes, Lukas? You know where they are." Mum whispers.

"Certainly." He rushes off and before I know it, all three of them are sitting around me on the sofa, ice cubes in my hand, trying to keep me away from that awful state of freeze. Somehow, it is working. I'm not entirely here, the dissociation is creeping in, but I'm not gone either.

Lukas gives me a brief, yet warm smile and asks: "Are you okay with us discussing our next steps or should we give you some time?"

"Discuss. We need to discuss it, it'll keep me here mentally." My parents lock eyes and nod in agreement.

"What is your professional opinion?" Mirek asks Lukas.

"It is quite clear we are no longer safe in Murcia. The killer has located Oliwia's residence and is resuming old patterns by murdering the people around her."

That was a bit unnecessarily straightforward, but alright. "Anyone who tries to get close to me, dies." I matter-of-factly blurt out. I feel so bad about how I treated Tanya. If I had stayed, maybe I could've prevented this.

"Pardon my language, Oliwia, but if we discuss our options, we need to leave emotions at the door for a moment." Crikey Lukas, this is a new side to you.

"Got it." Is all I can retort to that.

"Now that the killer has struck again, we need to take you all to a place where there is an entire team working around the clock to catch them."

"You're saying Brussels." Dad adds.

"Yes, I believe it is time to go home."

"And then what?" Mum asks. "Wait until he strikes again? Can't we go into hiding someplace else?"

CHAPTER 13

"No!" I yell out. "No more hiding. You see what good that did. We have to finish this. *I* need to finish this."

"I want you to guarantee the safety of our child." Mum pleads.

"I cannot guarantee anything, but at least there we'd have an entire operation rather than just me."

"A manhunt."

I cringe at my dad's comment.

"Or personhunt? Is that more appropriate?" Bless him.

Lukas' phone goes off. Great, what else?

"Excuse me, I need to take this." He walks off into dad's office without even asking. I can tell Mum isn't exactly happy about that move either.

"What?" Dad lifts his shoulders. "This is his home too."

A couple of minutes later Lukas walks back in, brushing his fingers through his long, wavy blonde locks.

"I'm afraid I have more bad news."

"Of course you do." As if I'm surprised. "What is it?"

He pulls out his phone from his pocket and hands it over to me. "I'm so sorry, Oliwia."

A video from the national news in Belgium titled 'Double homicide in Europea Halls' flashes at me. My parents come round and stand behind me. Their support means the world, but in the end I always end up alone somehow. Have you ever been in a room full of people, but felt so devastatingly alone? Everything has been set in motion. I knew it'd happen, but still – I'm not ready. How could I ever be?

I press play.

Shots of the main gates of Europea Halls, barred off from

spectators by police tape. "Nearly two years after the horrific massacre at Europea Halls, the residents have once again been shaken to their core as a young woman named Saskia Berevoets and a local guard at the halls called Fabrizio Aiello have been found dead in the upstairs library. The police have ruled out suicide and have not yet commented on a possible connection to the killings that happened in Budapest last summer."

There's more, but the rest is not registering. Saskia. I haven't talked to her in two years, but I was close to her in the movie club. She was always so kind to Karla and me. And Fabrizio, a nice yet cocky guard at the halls. What's the connection between the two? Some shots of the halls' gardens and Europea follow up, together with a photo of me and my friends. All lined up like a school yearbook, except that they're all dead. The moment the video mentions my name, my mum puts her hand on my back for moral support. I can feel her heavy breathing. This isn't easy for them either. Then I'm pulled back to the screen. Jelena? Why are they interviewing *her*?

A teary-eyed puffy mess, Jelena looks straight at the camera, through the screen, burning into my soul. "Saskia was my best friend. I have no idea who this Fabrizio is, but I do know there must be a connection to Oliwia. Liv-" I'm taken aback that she still calls me that. "If you see this message, please come home. I urge you."

That's a lot of information to digest, all at once. Not like I haven't been here before, but certain things you never get used to. Tanya, Saskia and Fabrizio, all dead because of their connection to me. Granted, they were never my best friends, but they were still good, innocent people who had their whole lives ahead of them. Cut short. Guilt is one of those nasty

CHAPTER 13

ones, creeping in when you think you're on the mend. I'm sure there's plenty of online trolls again on socials; good thing I don't have any apps anymore. Still, I shouldn't care about those cowards. I know that, rationally. But there's a whole lot of rationale missing these days.

"Why would that girl urge you to come home? I haven't even seen her before."

"That's Jelena, Mum, another friend from the movie club. We all used to hang out together a lot, the Europea Halls crew and them."

"So she knew the other victims too?"

"She did. She was never as close to them as I was, but we did all go out together. To that Great Gatsby night, for example."

"Oh, I do remember you looking ravishingly gorgeous in that Art Déco patterned dress."

I chuckle. "Thanks, I guess?"

"I still don't understand why she'd be so direct as to calling you home. It's not her place to ask."

"I'm a bit dumbfounded by that too, but then you could see she'd been crying. It might've been an emotional response, she probably wants answers just as much as I do. Saskia was her best friend. Since childhood."

Ping.

That sound - it always startles me. No text message will ever feel safe.

"Who is it?" Dad reacts.

"Hold on."

Balazs: *Good luck on your non-date tonight! Let me know how it went! Love u, x*

"It's Balazs, asking me about how things went with Tanya."

"He is just the nicest young man, isn't he?"

For once, I agree with Mum. "He really is."

"A shame he doesn't appreciate sexual intercourse."

"Holy - Mum, you can't say those things!"

She stumbles as Lukas cracks up. "I only meant to say he is a very attractive young man, it almost feels like a waste of beauty."

"You're digging your own grave there, Basia." Dad is laughing too now.

"I swear, you're lucky I know you or you'd be cancelled by now." For someone trying to act so proper, she can be so impossibly rude at times.

"Fine, I'll behave. Anyway, darling, you should tell him what has transpired here."

I look back at my screen, my heavy heart not convinced as to what to do. "The thing is, he's back in Budapest."

"Your point being?" My dad replies.

"Perhaps we can keep him safe by not saying anything. I've lost almost everyone around me, I can't bear the thought of losing him too."

"Don't you think you'd want to know if you were in his position?"

"Don't you know I despise rhetorical questions, Lukas?"

He grins. Mum's eyes are about to drop out of their sockets with horror at my comment.

"Sorry, I'm sorry. That wasn't necessary. I want to protect him, that's all."

"Then tell him to come to Brussels too. Him and his family

CHAPTER 13

can have all the police protection he needs. He is easy bait at this point, not having any protection around him in Budapest. You know the killer comes after the ones you love. All of us should stay together."

I hate that he makes a good point. I'm still conflicted though. "Alright, I see where you're coming from. Listen, tomorrow morning he has his Master's dissertation and after that he will have graduated. Let him have that moment first. I'll call him right after, then he and his family can join us in our home in Brussels. The killer was spotted here tonight, there's no way he'd make it to Budapest by tomorrow morning."

"With all due respect, Oliwia -" that's never a good start to a sentence. "You know very well that there is a possibility there are multiple killers out there. Both LeBeaux and Karel had accomplices, so perhaps there is someone ready to strike in Budapest as we speak."

He's getting on my last nerves now, but I know he's right. "Let's do it this way: you call your team and ask them to have protection around the university and have someone follow him on his way there tomorrow morning without him knowing. That way he gets to have his moment before - before reality sets back in."

Lukas agrees. "That's a good idea, Oliwia. Then at noon you can call him and ask to take the first flight over."

"Commercial?" Mum gasps.

"What else?" Lukas replies.

"Absolutely not. Who knows where the killer could be hiding. If we take our private jet tonight, the pilot can rest enough to pick up Balazs and his family by tomorrow noon. I will not treat that poor man like a plebeian."

"That's" almost "very kind of you, Mum. Thanks."

"That's agreed then. Mirek, call Joseph. Tell him to get the jet ready. We're going home."

Chapter 14

ABELINA

The early morning rays illuminate the apartment and hit the roof of the Parliament on the other side of the river. It's a crisp January morning. I knew it was the right fit for the three of us the moment I saw that view for the first time. I had never lived in the capital before, so moving away from lake Balaton was a terrifying, yet exciting move. There was no way I'd leave my son to his own devices. He might say he wants to be independent, but I also know how co-dependent he and Szofi were. He'd never been the type before who would start hyperventilating. I wish I could take the hurt away from him, but I have my own scars as well. As a single mother to twins, life hadn't always been smooth sailings. However, nothing could've prepared me for losing one of them. That kind of loss is unfathomable. You hear about all these people that grow apart through the grieving process. At least it has brought him and I closer together. Is it a healthy mother-son relationship? Perhaps not, but nobody tells you how to pick up your life after it's been smashed into pieces.

I stare at Szofi's pictures on the coffee table. I feel her presence around the apartment, around the city, wherever I go. I do believe she's with us. I know I won't heal, but Balazs is younger. He might find a way out of the grieving, eventually. That's all I can wish for him really.

Balazs steps out of the bathroom, looking sharp in his suit.

"You look great, Son."

"Thanks, Mum." He gives me a peck on the cheek and picks up his suitcase. When did he turn into an adult?

"Your aunt should see you like this! She'll come back in the evening, can I take a photo?"

He rolls his eyes at me and then complies. I suppose some things never change.

"Gorgeous!" I'm starting to get a little mushy. "Szofi would've been so proud of you, Balazs."

"Today is for her." We both look at the frames on the coffee table filled with memories.

"And for you. You've worked very hard at this. I'm so delighted for you. Celebrate yourself today, know that whatever happens at the dissertation, you've given it your all. That's all anyone can do."

"Go on then, let's take a photo together."

"Really?" That's so sweet of him, I know how much he hates selfies.

"Really. Come in here." He gives me one of his big bear hugs and takes a couple of photos on his mobile. "Well then, time for me to head out, mum. Wish me luck!"

"The best of luck, Son. You've got this."

I give him another hug and wave him goodbye. The sun is shining on the dancing Danube. Today is a good day. He's earned it.

Chapter 15

BALAZS

Today is for you, Szofi.

I open up the main gates to the apartment complex and breathe in the city smells as the sun welcomes me. I stroll across Margit bridge, Margit island greeting me on the left side. It's still full of tourists during the winter season, even this early on. There's bikes and steps everywhere on the island. The musical fountain is swaying along to the classical music. I know it's a bit of a tourist trap, but I'm a sucker for fountains. In the evening there's an entire light show that accompanies the music and the rhythmical movement of the water jets. Szofi and I used to hang out here sometimes, just because. We'd do some tourist spotting and guess where everyone was from. The Australians and Americans are the easiest to spot, that's a given.

I continue down to the other side of the bridge, taking in the magnificent sight of the Parliament with its hundreds of turrets. As I walk around the imposing building, more memories flood me. Today is a special one. Szofi and I would often hang out at Szabadsag Square too, especially when the football matches were being projected on the screens. During the World Cup, there was a really cool vibe. We met so many people during those games. I was usually the one doing most of the talking, but she assured me she liked it that way. Szent Istvan Bazilika's dome is towering over the side street I head down. In one way, it's been really practical to live so much closer to the centre, just next to the bridge on the Buda side, but it doesn't feel the same. I wonder if Budapest will ever be my home again now that she's gone.

I walk down Arany Janos street until I see the Brutalist university building in front of me. Let's do this.

There's an odd sensation of being watched that rushes over me. I glance over my shoulder and a man in a suit looks away, and I think I've seen him before, at the bridge earlier in the day. My dissertation on PTSD reminds me of how paranoia plays a part in the trauma processing phase. This is a sign, surely.

Another Master's student is about to sit down next to me in the waiting room, but I kindly ask him to save the seat next to me. He acts a bit stupefied, but assents to my request in the end. Always leave a seat for the dead. She's here next to me in spirit.

I pull out my phone and am about to text Oliwia, until I notice she hasn't been online in hours. She probably needs her sleep. I'll text her right after.

"Balazs?" A middle-aged bored-looking woman peeks her head out of the auditorium room. "We're ready for you."

I scan the room as I enter and notice the six jury members at the back of the large, hazily lit auditorium. This is all a bit pompous, them sitting way back there for my presentation. The man I spotted outside is standing by the back door. That's weird. He looks like some sort of a security guard. Since when do they have a budget for that at this uni?

CHAPTER 15

I step onto the small podium and plug my laptop into the USB cable, connecting it to the large projector.

"If you need any help, we can get our IT staff in." One of the male jury members responds in a monotonous tone.

"That's okay, I think. Thank you." I notice my right hand is trembling as I am trying to connect the cable to the correct portal. My throat and lips have suddenly turned as rough as sandpaper. Water, you forgot about that one. I cough to release some of the stress and phlegm.

"Would you like some water?" A kind older lady from the jury asks.

"Oh, yes please, I'd love that."

She walks down the broad staircase of the auditorium as I continue setting up. As I am finishing up, the lady pours me a large glass of water, nods politely as she hands it to me and returns to her throne. I log onto the Cloud and download the PowerPoint presentation. I glance back at the guard in the back, who has a nervous mystique about him. Focus on your screen. The light of the projector turns on and the dusty, tiniest of particles hover around the large beam. I've got this.

The first eight slides go better than expected. Once I had a big gulp of water, the rest followed naturally. I imagine Szofi is sitting in the front row, cheering me on. The jury's stoic faces don't give away much, but I know I am doing alright. Graduation is just around the corner, after five years of studying. The first sign of normalcy is awaiting.

"On the next slide, you can see the effects of intergenerational or transgenerational trauma, as has been discussed by BC Bradfield in his 2013 study. If you have a look at these statistics-" I press on the next button.

A photo of Szofi and me appears on the screen.

I take two steps back and try to compose myself. "I do apologise. That wasn't supposed to be in the presentation." The jury members look at each other and scribble down some notes. "So sorry, this is my twin sister who passed away half a year ago. Perhaps it's not a coincidence she's here." I try to make the most out of a bad situation. As long as they don't think I'm throwing a pity party, that's the last thing I'd want to do. My chest is closing down, making it a bit harder to breathe deeply. "Should I continue to the next slide or is-?"

"We are truly sorry for your loss, Balazs." The kind old lady speaks up. "We had heard about this some months ago, but wanted to give you the time to process things at your own pace. I believe *we* are the ones who should apologise here for never having checked up on you. We are psychologists after all. I believe we have failed you. My sincerest condolences. By the way, that is a beautiful photo of you two together." The other jury members acknowledge her words. A tear finds its way down my right cheek. My mum always says support can turn up out of the most unexpected of places. The woman can see I'm upset and continues: "Will you be okay to do the rest of your presentation, young man, or would you like us to reschedule?"

I straighten and pull my shoulders back. "I will be okay. Thank you so much for those touching words. It means -" my voice cracks, "Excuse me, it means a lot. Okay, so, on the next slide we can have a look at the statistics of transgenerational trauma therapy."

A photo of Szofi's bloodied beheaded body pops up on the projection screen.

Revulsion hits hard. I hear multiple gasps and a tiny scream from the back row. I hide behind my hands and pretend this

CHAPTER 15

isn't real. How is this even possible? I peek back and notice it's a photo taken inside the building where she was killed. This was taken by the killer, no doubt.

"Young man, care to explain what –"

"I have no idea." Sweat starts forming in my arm pits. "I- I don't know what to tell you. That's - that's my sister." I start crying. First softly, then louder. The killer is ruining my life again, knowing very well how important today is. Seeing her body on display like this, zoomed in on her neck, is beyond distasteful. I try to shut down the slideshow, but click next instead. Big letters show up this time.

WELCOME TO ACT THREE.

Oliwia was right: it wasn't over yet. I start hyperventilating as these dooming letters are even worse than seeing my sister's headless body.

The man at the back door starts walking towards me. What's going on here? Should I run?

"Who – who are you?"

"Calm down, Balazs, I am a policeman."

"You should know, telling someone to calm down when they're stressed never works." I blabber.

"I was asked to come here today to protect you. Jury?"

The old lady is the first one to reply again. "Yes, Balazs - sorry, we didn't want to upset you in case this was a false alarm. We're so extremely sorry."

Sorry doesn't begin to describe my emotions. How could they put my life at risk like this, if they knew something bad could happen? More importantly, why would they put themselves at risk? This doesn't make any sense.

"Oliwia-"

He knows her name.

"- wants to talk to you. You should call her. I will accompany you."

"Accompany me? Where to?"

"I suggest you make that call first. I'll be right here."

Chapter 16

OLIWIA

My mum, Dad and Lukas all look at me, gazes full of impatience. We're sitting on the sofas of our townhouse in Brussels.

"That was Balazs."

"Oh darling, is he okay?"

"No. He sounded like he was in shock. Someone messed with his presentation. It included a photo of Szofi's dead body with the text 'Welcome to Act Three'."

My dad's mouth falls open.

Mum rolls into protective mode. "That poor man! We need to get him over as soon as possible. Luckily we've made it back in time. Mirek -"

"I know, I'll call Joseph."

"It's really happening again." Anxiety shoots through me, an all too familiar sensation. "A part of me had hoped he'd be spared this time."

My mum hugs me. "We're in this together, Oliwia. Nobody's going to hurt you this time around."

"You can't make empty promises like that, Mum."

She tilts her head back. "I'm sorry. You know what I mean."

"I do. Balazs was going to call his mum and aunt. He's on his way to the airport with the policeman. Lukas, could you please check who tampered with his presentation? Perhaps someone on your team could check the IP address to find out who is behind all of this."

"I was about to suggest that, Oliwia, great idea."

Ping. Another text. Take your time, exhale. It's probably Balazs.

Balazs: *My mom and I are about to board. Thanks so much for arranging this. My auntie's not joining, she's never been outside of Hungary and wants to hold down the fort. I'll see you in three hours, Liv. Hang in there. x*

"Balazs and his mum are on their way. His aunt isn't coming."

"That's rather worrying. Did she say why?"

"She's never left Hungary and I guess she's not about to now."

Lukas speaks up. "I'll make sure we keep an agent around their apartment until all of this is over."

"Thanks, Lukas."

Until all of this is over. Whatever that might mean. Something does feel final this time around. The closing chapter in a slasher trilogy. It always goes back to the beginning. So here I am, back in Brussels. I crack my right wrist and hold onto my pocket knife. Bring it on, I'm not going down without a fight.

Chapter 17

JELENA

The thick mist hangs low between the pine trees, almost like an impressionist painting. The air is moist and cold, the smell gradually waking me up. It's far too early, I'm still catching up on sleep after all the obligatory January family parties. I'm deep in the Zoniënwoud, the largest forest in Belgium, right underneath Brussels. The light blue seamlessly flows into the pastel greens of the dewy pine needles.

I check the location on my phone again, Erik is close by. He rang me up early this morning, his voice shaky, stating he had info on Saskia's death. I had to come alone, I had to promise him. Something about that smells fishy, so I did tell my dad where I was going. You never know.

Socials have been going bonkers regarding Saskia's murder. I don't think I've had any time to digest the news, this all appears more like a nightmare. I hope I get answers today, so I can take the time to grieve. She was my best friend. I've known her since I was five. It's always been her and me against the revolving-door city of Brussels. People kept coming and going in our friend circle, that's the way it is here. All those diplomats and Euro-bubble expat families don't hang around for too long. Most don't even give Brussels a proper chance. They work at the EU institutions, come home and pretend they know the city and moan about it. It does my head in. They only know the square around the institutions, but are not in touch with the actual city at all. Anyway, rant over. What I meant to say is that Saskia is one of the few who stuck around. One of the few other local Flemish people, along with her brother Erik. Losing her has been too surreal to even try to grasp.

There he is. Erik throws me a downcast look. The mist disperses as I walk in his direction.

"Erik, hey." I give him a kiss on the cheek.

"Hey, Jelena." His dejected voice shows I'm not the only one who's lost someone.

"Why did you want to meet here?"

He peers around nervously. "I wanted to guarantee we'd be alone. Nobody is ever here at this part of the forest this early on."

"Why not at your apartment?"

"Those walls are as thin as cardboard. Nobody else can know, for now."

The tremor in his voice is not putting me at ease one bit. What is he so secretive about? "Go on then, what do you know about Saskia's murder?"

He is about to speak, but closes his mouth again. He peeks at the thick tree trunks behind me. I turn back and inspect the foggy trees. "What are you looking at, Erik?"

"I'm not - I don't know how to do this."

"Take your time. She was your sister."

"That's not what I mean." A sorrowful look, almost pitiful, makes me wobble. Something in his eyes is different today. They're vacant black pools. "It was never supposed to go like

CHAPTER 17

this."

"What do you mean? Just tell me what's up Erik, you're making me nervous."

His gaze goes back to the trees behind me. "What do you keep looking at?"

"My sister was never supposed to die. That wasn't part of the deal."

I take an unbalanced step back. I don't think I should have come here today.

"The - the deal? Which deal?"

He lowers his head and exhales dramatically slow, his shoulders drooping. "It was wrong to bring you here."

The impending sense of doom mixed in with the misty setting around me makes me feel trapped. My legs stuck in quicksand, the longer I stay, the higher the chance I'll be swallowed up alive.

"Erik - You need to tell me *now*, or I'm leaving."

He lifts his head with a brisk move, an unnerving darkness in his eyes. "Leave."

"What?"

"Get out now, *run!*" His yell travels through the forest, echoing through the branches, startled birds flying off into the morning skies. I want to move, but I still don't get what is happening here.

Behind me I notice the rustling of leaves. I pivot and spot black boots; a hooded figure with that mask I've seen all over the news, carrying a large chainsaw. An instinctive cry releases as the shape turns on the chainsaw, the aggressively brutal sounds juxtaposing with the peaceful scenery around us.

"I said get out! Now!" Erik positions himself next to the killer, who doesn't even seem to be bothered by his presence.

He obviously knows Erik. I don't have a single clue what the hell is happening here, but that's it. I'm out.

I sprint through the deep forest, hearing the chainsaw rattle behind me. I cut through the pines, zigzagging through the trees to shake off the killer. If I move past thicker branches, the chainsaw could get stuck. *Run to the chalet at the end of the forest, you can make it.* The sound isn't following me though. The killer is staying put.

I stop for a split second to orientate myself. I can still see the figure. Erik is holding him back, pulling his left shoulder as the killer is holding the chainsaw with his right hand, hurling it into the sky. I hide myself behind one of the broad tree trunks, peeking carefully to see what is going on.

The killer forces himself free from Erik's grip and lowers the chainsaw into Erik's left shoulder, cutting off his entire arm. I put my hand over my mouth, barely holding in the acid reflux. His arm drops to the leafy floor, blood spouting out of his shoulder. Erik's cries scare away more birds. It doesn't even look like he's trying to escape. He's staying put, no fight in him. The chainsaw bursts through the other side, another arm falling off lifelessly. Erik drops onto his knees. He's saying something now to the killer, but I can't make out what as they're too far away. His face looks pale, full of sweat. I should look away, but the curiosity in me is just too strong. He's not protesting, he was part of it. Could he have killed his own sister? If he knows the killer, to what extent was he involved with the murders in Europea Halls and Budapest? He was investigated by the police months ago for sending a so-called prank text to Oliwia. Not too sure that was a prank, looking at him now.

"Do it!" He shouts, chills run down my spine as I hear the devastation in his fragile voice. The killer pulls Erik's hair,

CHAPTER 17

exposing his neck to the chainsaw. This is too much. Let it be over with. The rattling chains tear through his neck, his dark bloodied head drooping down behind his body. The mutilated body quivers, like a headless chicken right after its decapitation. It gives the impression of being in a fictional world, reality too absurd to cope with.

The entire forest goes back to its previous silence. The killer treads off calmly, no sign of fear or remorse in his body posture. He's not even looking for me.

I lean my head back against the rough trunk, grounding myself. My chest aches and it's only now that I notice how tense I've been. I need to tell Oliwia. Whatever the hell I've witnessed, it must be connected to her. I need a moment. I've never seen a dead body, let alone watched someone get brutally murdered. How does Oliwia do it, get through life after all those losses?

Chapter 18

BALAZS

Leaving my auntie behind makes me uneasy, but there was no persuading her. I had to hold my mum's hand the entire flight, this being her first. I wish it were under different circumstances. If there's anyone who deserves a holiday, it's her. She's worked so hard her entire life to provide for Szofi and me, she's never had the chance nor the money to take a flight somewhere. The furthest she's traveled is Slovakia and Romania, and that was for work. When the jet sped up for take-off, I felt the cold sweat on her hands. I talked her through the entire logistics of flying. It distracted me from thinking about what we're about to be confronted with. For those three hours, all there was to the world was my mum and me, surrounded by thick clouds. I check the time when we land, it's just past five in the early evening. It's already becoming a bit dark outside. I wish we could stay inside, because I'm all too aware of the fact that the moment we step out, life will hit us hard.

Oliwia and her parents are at the ready for us, standing by the limousine next to the private landing strip. The tension I've been holding in releases right there and then when she runs up to me and gives me a hug. We both sob into each other's arms. All the grief and fear of the past few months have an emphatic

CHAPTER 18

home in her arms. I don't want to let go. It's her and me, for a brief moment in time. I knew I'd missed her, but holding someone can bring back so many memories, so much love too.

"I've missed you so much, Liv." I can just about put into words how I feel.

"Me too. I wish -"

"Different circumstances, right?"

"Exactly."

"I know, but here we are."

I suspect we've been embracing for a while. When we finally unlock our arms, I notice my mum and Oliwia's parents are all drying their tears. My mum is shifting a bit awkwardly around them, not exactly knowing how to act in the situation.

"Mum, this is Mirek and Basia".

"I know, Son, we've introduced ourselves to one another." We must've been hugging for ages, I had no clue.

Liv signals to the man waiting by the limo. "That's Lukas over there."

He marches up to me and shakes my hand. Don't Belgians give kisses? Oliwia was right, he is a very handsome man. He's got very refined features. I instantly observe his energy: steady, warm and welcoming.

"Welcome, Balazs. I will do my utmost to ensure safety for you and your mother in Brussels." I'm not a fan of empty promises, but I'll take the intention. "Is everyone ready to go to the estate?"

"Estate?" My mum blurts out. She hooks arms with me and whispers: "You didn't tell me they live on an estate."

"I mean, what did you expect when we were picked up in a private jet, Mum?"

"Still, I feel so underdressed. Have you seen what that Basia-woman is wearing?"

"This is not a competition, Mum. They live a bit differently to us -"

"A bit?"

"But they're good people. They're not here to look down at us. They're here to shelter us."

"Ah great, I've always wanted to be a charity case." She replies ironically.

"Mum, give them a chance please."

She sighs exasperatedly. "You're right. I made this about me when it's not. I get self-conscious, you know me."

"I do, we're in this together, okay?"

She pinches my arm and steps into the limousine. "Time for our private tour." She grins kindly. "Might as well enjoy the city views."

The warm evening lights of the city tries with all its might to give me a hearty reception, but none of the beauty is truly registering. My mum appears more impressed. All I keep looking for is some sort of a glimpse of that mask. The mask I've been pushing away from my thoughts since I lost Szofi. That ungodly mask devoid of any human traits. I know it's only a matter of time before I'm confronted with it again. I just pray I didn't make a mistake bringing my mother here.

Chapter 19

OLIWIA

I can tell Abelina is impressed by the sights around her. We're about to pass the Atomium. I can already see the metallic balls lit up gorgeously at night.

"That's the Atomium."

"I've heard about it. What is it exactly?"

I turn on my 'Ingvild knowledge' button, anything to fill this oppressive silence.

"It was built in 1958 for the World Expo. Those nine balls represent the different provinces of Belgium."

"Aren't there ten?" My dad adds.

"There are, but at the time there were only nine. Anyway, the metal structure represents an atom, hence the form." I'm nowhere nearly as good as Ing at this. No future as a tour guide for me.

"I see. It looks quite tall."

"Over a hundred metres if I remember correctly. You can enter the balls by the way, it's a bit like a sci-fi movie from the inside, with some psychedelic escalators in there."

"Is it some sort of a museum then?"

"I haven't been inside in ages, I think so. There are great view points up there and a restaurant on the top ball."

"Oh, it must be lovely up there."

We run out of pleasantries and fall back into quietude.

Balazs takes hold of my hand. "Thanks for that, I know what you're doing."

I smirk. "I want to make sure she feels okay. To whatever extent that is possible."

"See, I told you. There's still so much kindness in you."

We drive past large boulevards filled with townhouses, the archetypal view of suburban Brussels. Ingvild used to tell me that she had mixed feelings about the architecture in the city. She said every single street was so eclectic in styles that at times she missed the Norwegian homogeneity of its cities. Now I get what she meant. There's a stunning Art Nouveau house, next to an imposing Neo-Classical one, next to a Functionalist apartment block that looks more depressing than anything I've been through. There's a lot to love and loathe here. This detached sensation of entering the city again yesterday made me wonder whether Brussels is still our home. If anywhere is our home. Wherever I go, I'm a stranger, a passer-by. I'm often not even at home in my own body, the dissociation has become more familiar than the sensations of my own gravity.

Lukas opens the door for us and brings us through the wrought iron gates. Balazs' mum is gawking at the large symmetrical gardens leading up to the main building of the estate. A part of me is uncomfortable throwing our blue blood in their faces like that, but that's not the point of them being here. I hope Balazs knows that too.

Chapter 20

ABELINA

I knew there were plenty of rich people in Brussels, but I didn't expect this type of wealth. The gardens almost look like a Louis XIV masterpiece, as if entering the Versailles grounds. Or is it Louis XV? I'm not as good at art as Balazs, but I know my fair share. I might not have travelled as much as these people, but I've educated myself in the few moments I had to myself over the years. A part of me wants to soak up as much as possible, but the fear of my son being in danger far outweighs any curiosity about being in Belgium.

As we enter the entry hall, the large marble staircase and chandeliers (yes, plural) wow me once more.

Basia walks next to me. "I do hope we shall be able to make you feel at home here, dear Abelina." Is she writing a medieval letter? Who talks like that?

"I shall try." I catch Balazs' smirk in front of me.

"Sadly we do not have our previous staff any longer, as we hadn't the faintest idea as to how long we'd be in Spain for."

"A home without staff? How do you manage?" Balazs turns around and frowns at me. He did ask me to give them a chance. I'm acting like a stubborn teenager.

Basia looks upset. Great start, I suppose it's not easy to push away the jealousy if I'm being honest. I've worked my ass off my entire life to provide for Balazs and Szofi and yet all I can afford is a small city apartment. And here I am, walking into what looks more like a palace than a house, money that has fallen into these people's laps purely because of generational wealth. They were born into it, I'm not even sure they work normal jobs. All of that doesn't matter now. We are all here for our kids. My pettiness has no place here.

"I'm sorry, Basia. That wasn't very kind of me."

She looks down at her shoes. "No, I am the one who's sorry. I do know I can rub people the wrong way. The last thing I want is for you to feel unwelcome here when your son has been such a pillar of strength to my daughter."

"We might not have much in common, but you and I are mothers." She glances back up, locking eyes with me.

"In all transparency, I have never met people from your - social class."

"I see, alright."

"So I became defensive. It makes me feel guilty that I can't provide this type of lifestyle for my children." I cough. "Child."

"Oh, darling, I am so appalled I'd make such a horrid impression!" I smile again, trying to ignore her accent. I do think she means well, there's just a bit of cracking the facade that comes first. "You are spot on, we're both mothers and if I am too direct, do tell me. I wanted to say I am sorry for your loss."

"That is very kind of you, Basia."

"May I -?" She shuffles towards me and gives me a hug. I am painfully aware of how reserved I am, so I try to mellow into it.

Chapter 21

OLIWIA

Balazs and I flop down on the velvet sofas. Dad is taking care of the fireplace and chatting away with Lukas as per usual.

"Did you see that?" I ask Balazs.

"Our mums? Yeah, I'm sorry. Mine can be a bit snarky around people she doesn't know well."

"No, I meant them hugging. It was nice. Slightly forced, but nice."

I lower my head onto his chest. It's nice to be physical with a friend without having to feel uncomfortable. He wraps his arm around me.

"Oh, that. Yes, they had a bit of a rocky start, but it'll be fine."

They both walk into the living room, arm in arm. I'm fairly sure my mum is forcing herself onto Abelina, but perhaps it's a nice feeling for her not having to cope with everything on her own. I can't even imagine what it's like losing your own child.

The fire starts crackling, subtly lighting up the dark oak panels of the living room. Our parents sit down next to us on the sofa, Lukas is hovering around the fireplace and making sure the fire doesn't go down.

"So, here we are." Dad's a master at stating the obvious.

"What's the plan?" I ask the group, not wanting to waste

any time.

"The corps has asked you and Balazs to come into the station tomorrow."

"No. Absolutely not." The others look surprised. "What? I've done that before, people ended up dead. If anyone wants to talk to me, they can come here."

Abelina nods. "I agree with Oliwia. We didn't come all the way here to go out there into the city centre and be lurked into a potential killer's lair."

"I understand. I'll ring the team now and ask them to come over first thing tomorrow morning. We could all do with some rest first." I'm glad he gets it.

He is about to walk off into the kitchen, phone in hand. "Lukas?"

"Yes?"

"Would you mind calling them in front of us?" As much as I *want* to trust him, I can't take any chances.

"Oh. Sure, no problem." The hesitation in his voice alarms me a bit, but he probably didn't expect that question.

"Good call." Balazs whispers into my ear.

All of us are completely quiet, trying to pick up what's being said on the other side.

"Yes, we would indeed prefer you to come here instead. Oliwia insists." He gestures an understanding look at me. "Okay, I do understand there are protocols to follow. We will be over say nine tomorrow morning?" Great, I forgot to tell him I'm not a morning person. Guess we're going to the station after all. Pick your battles. "Yes - what is it? Jelena?" My mum sits up straight, antennas up. "I see. I will run it by Oliwia. Jan - I need to ask you-" Jan. That name rings a bell. Didn't he work together with LeBeaux? "Call me the moment there are updates. How am I only hearing this now? I'm the one who's with the families, I should be the first to find out." Annoyance kicks in, he's *not* happy. "Exactly. Alright, notify me if there are any developments."

He sits down on an armchair opposite the sofas. All of us are eagerly waiting for the undoubtedly gut-wrenching updates. I can't take the silence any longer. "So they didn't agree to coming over, I suppose. I heard the name Jelena, is she okay?"

"Who's Jelena?" Balazs asks.

"She was a good friend of mine at a movie club Karla and I used to go to."

"Just Karla?" Lukas adds.

"No. Well, yes. Her and I went to all the meetings, but the entire gang from Europea used to join us for movie nights in Ixelles."

"So they all knew Jelena?"

"They did. Not as much as Karla and I did, but let's just say they were acquaintances."

"Did Karel and Lucija ever tag along?" He continues his questioning. I'm getting more worried by the second.

"They did, a couple of times. Lukas, what are you getting at? What happened?"

He takes a moment to compose himself, professional mask on. "Jelena came into the office earlier today. She saw Erik being killed. The murderer fit the description; black hood, white mask, black boots. A long blue overcoat."

Everyone gazes at me, checking in on how I'm taking the news. Balazs wraps his arm a little tighter around me.

Abelina interjects. "Erik? I'm sorry, but I'm not following."

I try to state the sentence as objectively and calmly as I can. "Saskia's brother, the girl who got killed. Erik used to hang out with us too, rarely, but you know - in the bigger friend circle. That is until he prank texted me after the murders in the halls."

"Are you sure it was a prank?" Abelina asks.

"I was, until now. Lukas, how did Jelena escape?"

"She ran off, hiding behind a tree. She was in the Zoniënwoud. She mentioned the killer was not even following her. Erik had asked her to come over and then said that his sister being killed was never part of the deal."

"The deal?" Balazs' voice is full of worry now, too.

"He was in on it. Somehow. The team is looking into it as we speak. He lured Jelena there, but then had a change of heart and told her to flee. That's when the murderer killed him."

"How was he-?" My dad asks.

"Don't." I respond. "I don't want to know. If any of you want to know about how and when and where, ask Lukas, but not in front of me." I have no interest in having more nightmares. As horrible as this is, I do not want to visualise how Tanya or Saskia died either. "Unless there are clues leading back to us in some way." I add, to be safe. "You know, I never trusted that Erik guy. He was a scrawny dude, so there's no way he was behind the mask, but it wouldn't surprise me if he were part of the entire operation in some way."

"Why wouldn't he be behind the mask?" My mum questions.

"Because of what I said, he was too skinny. The killer has broad shoulders and is way taller too. I saw him, mum, he was like an unstoppable killing machine." The flash of that imposing stature creeps me out to no end.

Lukas steers the conversation back to the situation at hand. "Jelena wants to see us at the movie club."

CHAPTER 21

"Us?" I'm confused.

"You, Balazs - and I would obviously accompany you both."

"Tell her to come here. Why would we go to that movie club?" Balazs asks carefully.

"Something about these murders. Saskia, her connection to Jelena, Erik. They were all involved, to some degree, with that movie club, with me. There might be some clues there. Something I've been missing all along." I hope Balazs gets what I'm trying to say.

My parents look unsure. Lukas catches their glances. "I would be with them at all times."

"Well, when does she want us to come?" I ask.

"Now."

I'm exhausted, mentally and physically. The thought of going all the way down to Ixelles at this point wears me out. "*Now?*"

"I guess there's no time like the present." My dad points out.

Abelina shuffles closer to us. "Son, do you really think this is a good idea? Heading off to some empty building when it's dark out? Is this even about you? No offense, Oliwia, but this all points more to you than to Balazs."

"Is any of this a good idea? How can we know until we get there?" He asks himself, blatantly ignoring the crude comment about me.

"Couldn't we all stay here and have a video call or something?" His mum is obviously not too convinced about any of this.

Lukas stands up. "I do believe Oliwia makes a good point. Perhaps we can find out more behind the killer's motive. It's worth a shot."

"It's not worth their lives though." Abelina jabs.

"This decision right here, this moment, is pivotal. From all the horror talk my daughter has been enriching my general knowledge with, I believe this is when smart people would shout 'stay, don't go!' and I'd like to think we are smart people." Mum's voice quavers, her eyes filling with tears. I get up and take her hands.

"I know how this looks, Mum. But don't you think we all deserve some sort of answers, closure even? What if Act Three is set in the movie club?"

She rolls her eyes at me. "You and your Act Three, you exasperate me."

"Because you know I'm right. It always goes back to the beginning. The movie club was Karla and I's beginning. Maybe it doesn't end in the halls."

"I will send over two policemen to ensure your safety here. They should've been here the moment we arrived, I told them we asked for back-up. Anyway, let me text them now quickly."

The doorbell rings, we all jump up, my mum and Abelina screaming.

Chapter 22

BASIA

Who would ring at this time in the evening? On a holiday? Who even knows we're back home?

"I'll get it, all of you - stay here." Lukas commands us. Somehow nobody protests. He grabs the gun from his back pocket. The entire living room is filled with utter fear.

We all sit there impatiently, our senses heightened by the potential of looming threat. The crackling fire is the only sound providing us with a false feeling of safety and homeliness. I keep scanning my family's faces, to see if they are hanging in there. Oliwia's lips are pursed, a tense grimace engrossed in the moment. Mirek is doing the same as me, he keeps throwing me "Are you okay?" glances, then back at Oliwia. She isn't responding. Her laser focus frightens me. How many times has she been through this? When will my darling ever feel safe again?

"Delivery!" The voice of a chipper woman echoes down the entry hall.

Oliwia frowns at me.

Oh, right. "Oh my actual days! The cheese board!"

"What?"

"I ordered a cheese board, remember Mirek darling? I wanted to make our guests feel welcome. Hold on, let me get that."

I get up from the sofa and spot Louiza at the entrance holding the board, Lukas glaring at me in disbelief. I hear a collective sigh behind me.

"You ordered cheese?" Lukas sounds like he's in shock. Has he never entertained people?

"Of course I did, I couldn't possibly let my guests starve after their long flight. Hello Louiza doll, let me have a look."

The presentation is impeccable. Blue, old, hard, soft cheeses embellished with dates, grapes and some black and white caviar. You know, just a little nibble. "Ah, you never disappoint. Send the bill to Mirek, would you, love?"

"Certainly. I added some lactose-free cheeses in there too, the older ones on the left, as you weren't sure about your guests' intolerances."

"Oh, delightful of you to think of that. This is why we hire you. Lukas, would you be so gracious as to take that heavy plate off of Louiza's hands?" I mean, it is bad enough I have to ask the young man. Some people have *no* manners.

I enter back into the living room, pulling out a loud "Tada!" accompanied by the compulsory jazz hands as Lukas presents the plate and puts it on the glass coffee table in front of the sofas. I'm not getting much of a response. Tough crowd.

"I thought we could all do with some snacks after such a long day."

Abelina's eyes are wide with wonder. "Wow, this all looks amazing."

"Louiza does know how to balance out a lavish cheese board, doesn't she darling?"

CHAPTER 22

"She does." Mirek forcefully agrees. He groans.

"This is so nice of you." At least Abelina shows some gratitude. Balazs digs in straight away, murmuring a shy "Thank you, Basia."

"Right, I do not want to distract from this gorgeous presentation." Lukas adds. Is he being cheeky? "But we should get a move on."

I exhale, deflated that I have failed to provide a moment of normalcy for all of us. "At least take some caviar with you, darlings. You can't go on an empty stomach."

Oliwia and Balazs take a napkin and put some cheese slices on top of them before they follow Lukas.

"Please -" They stop and look over their shoulders. "Please. Be careful. We love you."

I hate not knowing if I am sending my child into the lion's den. Impulses come up. "I should join you!"

"Mum, no." Oliwia walks back, hands the napkin filled with cheese over to Balazs, and takes my hands. "I get it. I do. You want me to be safe, but the harsh reality is that I'm not safe anywhere until we catch this killer or killers. I'm a tough cookie."

A tear glides down my cheek. "Oh, I know you are, darling. But why can't I join you? There's safety in numbers."

"You've done so much for me. The killer has never come after our parents, so it is my duty to keep you safe, too." Right then I spot two older policewomen entering the grounds. "There, see? We'll all be safe." I know she doesn't believe that either.

Chapter 23

LUKAS

I'm back on chauffeur duties. I do sympathise with the family. Their entire staff quit the moment they knew they could be in danger. When the chauffeur heard about what had happened to Ayat's driver, he was the first to leave. And here I am now, part butler, part chauffeur, and if there is some time left: part cop.

Balazs and Oliwia are gobbling down the cheese in the back seat. I don't understand how they can be hungry right now, my entire stomach is clenched up. Basia wasn't lying about Balazs. He is stunning. He exudes this aura of mystique and warmth at the same time. Perhaps I'll have some time to talk to him properly, us both being on the aromantic spectrum. Crazy how much has changed over the past ten years. I wish I could feel as free as he does, but I don't think most of my colleagues would be very accepting. The people I did try to come out to at the station chuckled and said: "So you're a horny gay guy who doesn't want a relationship, basically?" It made me not want to explain any further. It's not up to me to educate everyone. There's that line that Oliwia keeps telling her parents. What is it again? Pick your battles. I've picked mine.

"How much further, Lukas?" Oliwia mumbles, mouth full of

CHAPTER 23

some local bio cheese.

"About ten minutes according to GPS. I have notified the corps, there will be back-up too. Four of them."

"That's great, thanks man." I know she's not a fan of the police, but she's not fighting the idea of back-up anymore. I suppose she's picked her battles too.

"Listen, you were talking on the phone earlier and I think you mentioned a guy named Jan?"

"I did, yes. Why?"

"He was working for LeBeaux, wasn't he?"

Balazs looks up, distracted from his cheese-fest for the first time since entering the limo.

"He was. He's a good guy, though, I can assure you."

"I've heard that one before. We all know she was working with a team."

"Jan would never -"

"Neither would Lucija and Karel. All I'm saying is: be careful with whom you trust."

Chapter 24

BALAZS

Well, this place isn't what I was expecting. When I entered Oliwia's place - or palace rather - I was stunned by the beauty around me. I mean, I know she comes from money, but it was like walking into an exuberant museum of some mad artifact collector. The Chinese cupboards, those insanely big chandeliers, the dark carved wood everywhere around me. You could tell by the way she flung herself onto the sofa that her house is like the most normal thing in the world for her whereas I felt a bit self-conscious even sitting down, becoming one with the interior. I'm glad she isn't a show-off about all of it, she didn't give me a 'grand tour' or anything (even though I wouldn't have minded one bit, I'm really curious to see the rest of her home), but just nestled against me. Showing that I am welcome.

This place, however, this movie club is the polar opposite of grand luxury. Those cold hospital-like light fixtures shine all too harshly on the old school chairs and the ceiling is made up of what looks like a bunch of yellowed cardboard squares pushed together. A couple of torn movie posters - mostly 80s and 90s action and sci-fi films - try to liven up the place, but it's no palace. It's barely any bigger than the living room of my

CHAPTER 24

apartment. I'm actually sort of surprised Oliwia and her gang would come here, but perhaps I'm prejudiced. Maybe this place felt like a bit of normalcy to all of them, a spot to hang after school and talk movies without anything pompous around.

Lukas walks in first, throwing me a coy smile. I'm not sure if I am reading the signals correctly here, but it does feel like he's been eyeing me up a bit. That sounds so arrogant, vom. He could also be trying to figure me out, see if I'm a trustworthy sidekick to Oliwia. Normally I'm the worst at noticing if someone is flirting with me, but this is more obvious than usual - at least, I think. Anyway, he is a beautiful man, there's no denying that, but he's barking up the wrong ace tree here.

Jelena runs up to Oliwia, flanked by four policemen who are all seated; she's looking an absolute state. The poor thing, I recognise that glare. She's watched someone be killed before her very eyes. I know what that does to a person. There's no coming back from that. The moment she reaches Oliwia, they both freeze for a split second. Oliwia balls up her fists in her long oversize sweater. Jelena comes in for an awkward hug and they give each other a kiss. It's the body language of long lost friends being thrown into a situation they couldn't have ever expected to be in.

"Oliwia, I'm so glad you're here!" Her runny mascara shows she's been crying. Her entire pale face does. The long unkempt dark brown hair is tucked behind her ears, falling unevenly on her shoulders. She looks up at me. "You must be Balazs." I walk up to them and give her a polite kiss, 'cause I know it's a thing here in Belgium. "A pleasure." What a dumb thing to say to a girl who's in complete disarray. I don't know what else to utter, so I look to my left and catch myself looking into Lukas' eyes. Great, even better. The ground, the ground is safe, look there. Lukas steps in her direction and introduces himself as well - in a far more elegant manner than mine, of course.

"I'm so sorry about Erik and Saskia." Oliwia blurts out. "So, you think he was in on it?" She's going straight for the jugular. No time to spare, I suppose.

"He must've been. He was fully aware the killer was hiding in the forest. He saved me alright, but I don't think that was his original intention." We all take a wobbly wooden chair and sit in a circle. Lukas, Jelena, Oliwia and me in the centre with the four policemen around us. "He had a chainsaw, Oliwia, can you believe it? A big-ass old chainsaw!"

Oliwia closes her eyes and exhales. "Is that how-"

"Yes, the killer cut off his arms and head. I saw it all happen, every stringy piece of torn flesh. It was - I can't even put it into words." Her eyes are still full of shock. I know Oliwia didn't actually want to hear any of that, but, too late now.

"I understand. Better than you can imagine. But the important thing for you is that the killer didn't come after you, if I got that right?"

"He didn't. I don't think I'm of any interest to him. So these four guys here, not necessary. I mean, thank you for your service or what is it they say?" The four policemen all smile. "I don't think this is needed though. I wanted to talk to you, 'cause you were always the horror buff of the gang."

"So were you."

"To a lesser extent, but yes, thanks. Anyway, I thought if we put our heads together, we could catch this freak before it's too late. I mean, no offense, you know what I want to say." Nobody knows how to word things in situations like these, that's painfully obvious tonight. Jelena raises her hand at me. "And how about you, Balazs? I didn't mean to exclude you. Do you know a thing or two about horror?"

"Afraid not. Just the real life kind." Way to be a Debbie downer, man.

"Oh, I see. Yes, I'm sorry about your sister."

That one never gets easy to digest. "I appreciate that." My shoulders tense up and I find myself clenching my jaws.

"How about you, officer Lukas?"

"Just Lukas is fine. I know a lot about detective series, you know - CSI and whatnot."

"Ah, the PG-13 version of horror. Well, you never know you might be able to help."

She's a bit of a direct one, talking to a policeman like that.

"You know what all of this means, right, Liv?" She calls her that, too?

"I'm afraid I know where you're going with this."

"You've found yourself in the closing chapter of a trilogy." My mind races back to the words 'Act Three', projected onto the large screen at my university hall. I need to listen carefully, whatever they know could be of vital importance if it comes to it. And I know all too well it will.

"A trilogy. I know. A part of me has been trying to decipher the tropes of a Slasher Trilogy, but there aren't that many to start with."

"What are you talking about, Liv? There's plenty! "Cold Prey" -"

"You mean "Fritt Vilt"? That last movie was a prequel."

"Fine. How about "I Know What You Did Last Summer"?"

"Hardly a trilogy, I doubt anyone takes that third part as canon."

"Or that series."

"Which was canceled after one season? I mean, my point exactly." They're losing me here. Let them geek out, they probably need it.

"How about "Scream" then?"

Oliwia is lost in thought for a while, biting the nail of her thumb. "It's become a franchise by now, but I guess the original three were seen as a trilogy."

"A bit like the "Halloween" franchise that has come out with the recent trilogy."

"Okay, so we have two decent examples. Any others we're missing?" Lukas is losing interest too now, or gaining interest as he's smiling at me. Floor. Look at the floor.

Jelena eagerly replies. "That recent "Fear Street" trilogy on Netflix! But then part three went back to Salem times."

"I haven't watched those."

"You haven't? Oh, you should!"

"I haven't really been in the mood for Slashers." Liv glances at me, a warm yet woeful look.

"I'm so clumsy sometimes, of course you aren't. So, "Scream". What can we learn from it?"

"That it always goes back to the beginning. The killer ended up being Sidney's brother and it all went back to the mother's murder."

"The beginning." I say out loud without even realising. "Do you think it'll end up in Europea Halls again?"

Liv nods. "Most likely. I have been mentally preparing myself to step back into those halls. I know it's only a matter of time." She's trying to sound strong, but the wavering in her voice says it all.

"What else is typical for the closing chapter?" I ask, because it is time to speed up the geek process a bit here.

Jelena is the first to respond. "They're often a bit more grounded, less chaotic than the first and definitely less of a body count compared to the sequel."

"That'd be a welcome change. What else?"

"What else, let me think. Oliwia, if you think of anything, by all means."

"No, go for it. I'm thinking."

"Okay well, something or somebody that you thought you knew all along from the first movie isn't what you thought it or the person was. Wait, I can word that better."

I smirk. "A twist."

"Oh baby, there's always a twist. It's probably so painfully obvious you'll kick yourself for not having figured it out sooner."

"What if it ties in to our families this time around?" Oliwia wonders.

"How so?"

"The mother in "Scream 3", the intergenerational trauma in "Halloween". You know, our families are here. Balazs' mum and both of my parents." That reminds me I still have to call my aunt when we get back.

Lukas speaks up. "Do you believe they're in danger this time around?"

Oliwia seems a bit surprised he is adding to the conversation now. "I - I sure hope not. It's bad enough that I've lost so many friends and my girlfriend. The killer does seem to have a certain demographic in mind."

"Ah yes, the promiscuous teen or young adult." Jelena winks at Oliwia. I guess she doesn't know I'm aroace either. I do appreciate Oliwia not telling everyone she knows. It shows I can trust her.

"Yes, well – mostly." A quick glance in my direction. "Also, the killer has murdered older people in Budapest and Brussels, but they were more in the way of his ultimate end goal. The lady on the Chain Bridge, Arpad, Ayat's driver. Generally speaking I don't think our parents are on the agenda."

"I hope it stays like that." I whisper.

"Me too, Balazs." Liv takes my hand and gently rubs it.

"So, what do we think will happen in the end? And how can we stop it?" A bit odd for Jelena to use 'we' like that, but I guess she means well.

"Well, it better not end up supernatural, I'd hate that." Oliwia laughs, an actual one. I'm as surprised as Lukas is.

"Or some sort of cult – or rich people paying for us to get offed." Jelena chuckles.

"Oh, don't even go there. The weird thing is, though, the killer almost felt supernatural. Who would survive all of that and still walk as if nothing has happened?" She's back to being serious, just like that.

"Michael Myers?"

"Well, there were definitely supernatural elements in that recent trilogy, from what I've heard."

"Maybe a young guy named Corey will take over."

I'm so lost right now.

"Or we'll end up in space."

"What? Oh right, "Jason X". Oh, this sucks on so many levels!"

"Could we–" Lukas hesitates. "Stay on track, please? I'm not really following anymore."

"Me neither." I add.

"Sorry, apparently it's easy to fall back into movie club

mode." Oliwia looks around. "It's this place. So many memories. Karla, the gang."

"Understandable. Let's summarise then." Lukas replies. "The final chapter is more grounded, perhaps connected to family ties, a big twist. Did I miss anything else?"

"Back to the beginning. Europea Halls. I'm sure it will all go down in Lovers' Lane. That's what the last message I received said."

"But the entire corps has raided that entire library. We couldn't find anything up there."

"You're missing something then. Or something has been planted there recently."

"Here's a crazy thought." I need to speak up, because all of our lives are on the line here. "What if we speed up the entire process and go there?"

"What, like - now?" Liv frowns.

"It's late now, we're way past midnight. Let's have a good night's sleep - if that's even possible - and head over tomorrow. If we know that's where they want us, then let's go there. We can have the entire corps come with us."

She nods. "That's not a bad idea actually. Why wait for the next one to fall when it's me he's after?"

That one still hurts to even think of. I know I got into this entire mess purely by bad luck - unless I'm missing something here - but through it all, she has become my best friend. I can't stand the thought of anything happening to Oliwia. Not after everything she's been through.

"I'm the Final Girl." She locks eyes with me. "They often do make it out alive, you know. This doesn't have to end badly." It's as if she can read my mind.

"She's right, Balazs. If she's made it through two movies,

there's no way the director is killing her off at the end."

"What about the rest of us?" I can't help but ask. "Are we all up for grabs, for emotional impact?"

"Let's make sure it doesn't come to that." Oliwia stands up and makes eye contact with all four policemen. "Tomorrow, Europea Halls, we're going back and we need all of you."

Chapter 25

LUKAS

We all make our way to the exit of the cinema club, the three young ones in front of us. I'm not entirely sure what the purpose of this entire geek fest was, but then again they might have needed a moment of physical togetherness to cope with all that's being thrown at them. I'm not convinced about any of those supposed trilogy rules either. They lost me at whatever "Jason X" meant.

The moment we open the door, the ice-cold January wind greets us mischievously. My colleagues walk up to Jelena and Stef asks her: "Do you want us to accompany you to your house, Miss?"

Jelena looks up at him and then turns her head towards Balazs and Oliwia. "Oh no, that won't be necessary." She points at a shabby old bike. "I'll bike home. Don't worry, I'm not taking public transport or anything. I've watched "Scream 6." No metros for me."

Oliwia grabs Jelena's hand as if by reflex. "Are you sure about that? You never know when the killer might pop up. I've learned a thing or two about splitting up."

"I'm sure, listen: he could've come after me today, but he didn't. There wasn't the slightest bit of interest. It literally takes me fifteen minutes to cycle home and I'm not stopping anywhere. I'm heading straight to my mum's." As tough as she sounds, her body posture isn't fooling me, there's definitely trepidation. "Look, if it makes you feel better I'll text you the moment I'm home."

"No. Don't text, call me."

"Why?"

"Anyone could text, I want to hear your voice." Smart cookie, that one.

"That's *such* a millennial thing to ask me." They both crack a smile. Way to make me feel old. "Fine, I'll ring you. Better yet, I'll video call you. Deal?"

"Deal. Be careful, alright?" Oliwia leans in for a hug and a kiss before heading for the limousine with Balazs and me. Stef and the others give me a polite wave and step into their police car.

Something ominous is hanging in the air tonight. All this talk of trilogies and final acts together with stepping into Europea Halls makes me wonder if tomorrow will really be the concluding chapter. I've been watching from the sidelines this entire time, but somehow I did end up becoming emotionally attached to Oliwia. It may not be the most professional move, but it's what happens after having lived together for months. I have this intrinsic need of protecting her at all costs, her and that Balazs guy. A part of me wants to have a chat with him tonight about being aro, but this is probably not the right time. Let's make it through the next few days first. I'm normally not the type to feel nervous or even anxious, but there is a part of me that is scared. I've gotten so close to Oliwia and her parents that I also could have become a target. Lord knows the guards

CHAPTER 25

in the halls didn't fare too well. I should have a good talk with Mirek, he'll get it. This isn't about me, it never has been, but I also don't want to end up getting butchered. Perhaps I should do a bit of karate tonight, to feel mentally-prepped. Remember who you are, man. You're a black belt top-notch policeman. No one has ever messed with me, why would it happen now?

Chapter 26

JELENA

I search for my earphones, but then decide not to wear them tonight. I should stay alert, just in case. It's only a short fifteen minute cycle though, get a grip. I put on my hat, gloves and scarf and set out for the trip.

As I set off to my mum's at the ponds of Ixelles, I try to focus on the road. I'm all bundled up, cause it's not the warmest of nights, but I don't mind this crispness. It's a quiet night, it's still a holiday, so most people are probably off to their native country or skiing somewhere in Austria or Switzerland. That reminds me of all the times I went to the Alps with Saskia. Or all the après-ski nights, I should say. We hadn't had a single fall out in all those years, we had always jelled without any competition or jealousy or whatever it is men think happens between women.

An Uber driver honks at me as he passes by, barely missing my front wheel. I brusquely stop, hearing the shouting of the driver becoming fainter by the second as he drives off. My scarf flies out of my winter coat when I hit the brakes. The entire world spins for a moment. The glimmering cobble stones of Brussels glare at me with warning. The stress I've been pushing down all day hits me all at once. Tears roll down my cold cheeks

CHAPTER 26

as I squeeze hard into the handles of my bike with my woolen gloves, hating this enormity of fear and heartache. I don't think I've actually started grieving Saskia yet, because I'm still in too much shock from what I saw with Erik this morning. Those blood splotches, those stringy pieces of meat flying around everywhere in the forest, those eyes rolling upwards into nothingness. Actually, I'm not even sure I'm in shock. I'm here, that's all I know. I need to get home. I balance myself and put my right foot back onto the pedal, kicking my frustration into the bicycle. I cycle a little faster this time, the sepia toned street lights and lit up buildings flashing by on both sides. It's a long street down towards Place Flagey, Ixelle's main square, and I let gravity take over, almost enjoying the rush of speed that overpowers the fear. I'm nearing the square and spot the hundreds of party goers. I knew there'd be people about, there always are. Doesn't matter which time of day, the place is always packed with people, even in winter. I hear the thumping electro beats approaching as I inch closer to the traffic lights in front of it. It's turning red, so I hit the brakes with all my might. A screeching sound hits the street, I definitely need a new bike soon. It takes me a couple of seconds before I come to a halt. A small smile erupts on my face as I see people in the dark, dancing and shouting something unintelligible in French. There's mostly francophone people in this part of Brussels, lots of Parisians move over 'cause it's a calmer lifestyle here and you can get more bang for your buck.

I hear a text-message alert. Oliwia is probably checking in already, bless her. I should check, I don't want her to worry. I take off one of my gloves and reach for my phone.

Unknown Number: *You talk too much.*

What the actual? The stress rolls back into my body, twice the strength. All those other people received text messages too from an unknown number, Liv told me about this. I need to get home. *Now.* This is bad news.

A pair of strong gloved hands pulls me off my bike and drags me into a quiet side street, away from the crowded square. I can't see who it is, but I can guess. I scream and flail my arms around, trying to get someone's attention. There's nobody in the street though. There are plenty of lights turned on in the apartments around, so if I keep yelling someone will surely come out. They must. I wriggle myself free from his death grip for a second and get a chance to look at him. That white demon mask. Those inhuman features, weathered by time, pierce through my soul. I thought I was safe. I should've known better. I want to run, but something inside me blocks me from doing so. The figure lunges at my throat and pushes down hard. I try to shout, but those hands are too strong. Squeaky, defeated tones of high pitched cries come out, too silent for anyone to hear. He pushes me onto my knees, his hands still firm around my throat. I smell the leathery gloves, almost comforting in a sick way. I look up at him, not wanting to lose consciousness. It's like razor blades cutting through me. Then I hear the most awful sound, worse than that chainsaw. Something inside snaps. Like crunched ice. I think I scream, but nothing comes out - absolutely nothing. He's crushed my vocal chords. I start shaking uncontrollably, gasping for air.

He lets go, finally. I drop down onto the moist cobble stones on all fours and inhale as much air as is humanly possible. I do this a couple of times, just in case the second round is coming next. I need air, I need to breathe. *You're still here, you're not dead.* The breathing doesn't come naturally though, my entire

CHAPTER 26

throat feels like it's burning and shut tight. Like a broken straw I try to drink through.

He lowers down to my height and pulls me back up. I notice his gloves are off now. Those look like male hands. There's no way this is a woman. He pulls out a pair of scissors. What does he think he's doing? I instinctively release a muted scream and as I open my mouth, he pulls out my tongue. I try to bite down hard on his knuckles, but he's pulled it out too far for me to hurt him. I frantically scan the apartments around me, but there's still no-one around. The drowned-out party sounds just around the corner throw me into deep despair. More tears. He takes the scissors and cuts into my tongue. The sharpest pain I've ever felt. I close my eyes, so I don't have to see what is happening. I taste the blood spilling in and out of my mouth as the cutting continues. I can tell part of my tongue is hanging loose. Fast, repeated, intense rhythmic cuts until I know it's too late. A muddled thud makes me open my eyes. I know what it is, but I still need to be sure. My entire stomach is clenched, knots wrapped around my insides. My purple, blood-soaked tongue is lying on the ground.

How do I escape? How can I get out? Run.

I turn around in the direction of the square and sprint off towards the crowd. The killer is following me, I can feel him breathing down my neck. The people are close, I can get to them. I wish I could call for attention, but I have no voice left and it's dark out. I ignore the horrific pain and move on, my legs going in full on power mode. I spot my house on the left side of the road behind the square, next to the pond. *Should I run home instead?* That's a bit further though. Too risky, even if it's only two minutes away.

The edge of the scissors pierces my coat, it pushes me to jolt even faster.

That's a miss, you bastard. I'm a mere seconds away from the crowd.

I can outrun him.

How is nobody even noticing us? Are they all too drunk and caught up in their own lives to look over their shoulders? Come on bitches, look.

The scissors crack through the back of my skull right above my scarf and under my hat. A light flash passes before my eyes and some odd coloured zig zags blind me for a split second. My knees turn wobbly, but before I get the chance to gather any strength I have left, the killer lifts me up and runs past the square, holding me. Some quick glances of people and a quick "Hey, are you okay?" from a gentle soul. I can't reply, it all goes too quick.

Where is he taking me?

The flashes come back before my eyes and a harsh headache is kicking in. I'm not sure which part of my body hurts more. He's heading for my house. He knows where I live. Somehow that scares me more than what's happening right now. I try to kick into his body or release myself, but my dangling feet just flap into the air, powerless. We move on past the last bit of the crowd, more people now starting to shout in the distance.

They're onto him. They'll help me. This can't be it, right?

He stops in front of my front door and rings the bell. *No, not my mum.* Leave her out of this, please, don't. He still holds onto me and pushes me back away from the door. What is he doing?

The pond.

He drags me across the muddy grass away from my front door and pushes me into the water. I drop down into the thick,

CHAPTER 26

ice-cold water and lose sight of where I am for a moment. The smell of moss invades my nostrils. I claw my way back above the surface and spot a couple of people from the square running in my direction. They're on their way. *Stay with it.* My head is above water, but I don't have the power to lift the rest of my body out. The broad-shouldered killer is towering over me menacingly. He almost looks supernatural, with the street lights illuminating his imposing stature. He's standing on the grass.

My mum, she's opened the door. "Hello? Who's there?" I vaguely hear. It's her voice, a hundred percent. A sinking feeling in my stomach warns me to prepare for the worst. *Please don't hurt her.*

She steps outside the door frame, looking left and right, wrapping her arms around herself to keep warm. I can see her through the killer's legs. Then she sees me too.

"Jelena?" She stutters. "B-baby? Is that you?"

I try to speak, but forget for a moment the state I'm in.

Her eyes stare at me. She has spotted the killer in front of me.

"Stay away from my girl!" She rushes to me. The killer pulls out the scissors and stabs me in my forehead. The flashes are back and I'm losing sense of my body. The fear makes place for sadness. He pushes my head under and water fills my mouth and lungs. Empty yells come out. I push back above water inhaling the steely air, hearing my mother's heartbreaking screams and the chaotic yelling of a gathering crowd. I can just about make out my mother punching into the killer. He pushes me back down, more water filling me up. I look above and see my mother fighting the killer. I try to keep my eyes open, but I can't. They're too heavy. I can't breathe. I grasp at my throat, trying to open it somehow. It's no use. *Please* let my mum make it out alive.

My lungs burst into my chest.

Chapter 27

OLIWIA

The short ride back home was filled with plotting; theories and whatnot. My mind was racing and Balazs tried to keep up with all my crazy ideas, bless him. When we entered back home, I decided to take a little moment to myself. Since we've come back to Brussels, I haven't really had a moment to myself. It's been investigations, meet-ups, socialising all the time. I need some time to recharge. I used to be the social butterfly, flying from group to group and introducing people to each other. I have noticed I need a lot more time to myself since everything that has happened. I don't have the same energy levels I had before. But that's fine, I can live with that. PTSD will do that to you.

I close my bedroom door behind me and plop onto my queen size bed. It's giving dark academia, Ingvild would say. I haven't received any texts yet, no unknown number or acronyms this time around. Things do feel different. Erik being killed when he seemed to have been part of it, it's as if the killer is preparing for the final battle and doesn't want any distractions around them. I'm ready, I think. It's odd, in Spain I was sort of living in limbo, awaiting the dreaded unavoidable, not really feeling that much.

I suppose that's what people call apathy. Being back is different. It's switched the analytical part of my brain back on, I'm not too sure about the emotional part though. I have this heavy block of concrete that's not fully allowing me to experience everything that is occurring and that is about to unfold. I'm very aware of it, so that's a good thing, but I'm scared of what it'll be like walking back into the halls. That's where life was at. The place I had my best moments with the girls. Somehow, no idea how, I've managed to keep my attacks pretty much under control, but there's this uneasiness sitting on my chest. My body is a ticking time bomb and I don't have the faintest idea when it'll be set off. I don't know if it'll be within my control or if I'll lose control. I've tried to be prepared, but how do you ever get accustomed to being in constant danger? Vera told me about chronically high cortisol levels and how it keeps the body in fight mode, but I also know it's not a sustainable way of living. That crash will come eventually. Not yet though, I need to stay with it. I keep seeing flashes of Lucija, LeBeaux and Karel, but they don't deserve my energy right now. The girls do.

I force my mind back into the halls, way back before the horrors started. Ingvild, Ayat, Marieke, Alzbeta and I are sitting on the yoga mats after our meditation session at Europea Halls. The teacher has just left and allowed us to stay here a bit longer, because our philosophy class is cancelled for today.

"So, what's she like?" Ayat blinks at me, eyes full of curiosity.

"Yes, spill the tea girl. You've been acting so mysteriously about her." Marieke adds.

"She's - I don't know where to start."

"From the beginning." Alzy smiles.

CHAPTER 27

"A very good place to start. When you read, you begin with -"

"Marieke, don't you dare start singing "The Sound of Music", I swear. I will lose it." Ingvild semi-seriously interjects.

"Then Liv shouldn't have taken me to the Movie Club. I had no idea I was missing out on such musical gold. I've been singing "Edelweiss" every day in the shower. That scene broke me."

We all laugh, a light breeze from the cracked open window flowing past us. It's early evening and the soft summer sun is beaming down on us. Ingvild's hair looks golden.

"Right, she's stunning."

"Of course she is, we wouldn't want an uggo for our Liv." Ayat jokes.

"That's a bit harsh! Anyway, I met her in the movie club. Well, officially met I suppose. I know she lives at the halls too and I had spotted her a couple of times before, but I had no idea she was -"

"A fellow geek?" Thanks Marieke. The eternal loud interrupter.

"If you want to put it that way. We started talking about DC versus Marvel."

"You're kidding me! She's into that as well? A match made in heaven!" Alzbeta is almost more enthusiastic than I am. Her dimples say it all.

I blush a little. "It is, we've been nerding out together."

"So, when are you introducing her to us?"

"I don't know, Ing, maybe it's too early."

"Why would it be? Don't you want to see how she is in a non-geeky social setting?"

"Ha, I suppose so. It would be nice to see if she gets on with you lot."

"Let's set a date then. Let me get out our shared calendars." Marieke opens up her phone and starts scrolling. The planner has awoken. "This Friday, we could meet her in your room. You said your roommates are out this weekend!"

"They are. I'm - I don't know, I guess I'm nervous. I've never introduced a girl to my friends before."

"There's a first for everything. If she's important to you, we'd love to meet her." Ayat pinches my elbow and gives me a cute wink. "Besides, I am failing my German class, I could use a little practice. Or is Austrian German very different from the German we see at school?"

"Ayat, girl, always thinking about your studies. You need to chill a bit." Alzy sighs.

"Oh, I know, I meant - nevermind, I'll go easy on her. But I did mean what I said, Liv, we want to meet her." They all nod in agreement.

My heart swells up with the love and acceptance from my girls. I don't think I've ever felt this happy, really. It was the easiest thing, coming out to them. Well, I can say that in retrospect. I was so damn nervous before telling them. The way they reacted though, as if it was a non-thing, in the best way possible. Seeing them sitting around me, inquisitive about my new girlfriend: it doesn't get better than this. These are my people and I'm the luckiest person in the world for having found them.

"Aw, Liv, are you tearing up?" Ing wonders.

I hadn't even noticed, but yes, I am welling up with pure gratitude. Ingvild comes in for a tight hug and gives me a kiss on the cheek. "I'm so glad for you, you deserve the world."

CHAPTER 27

The concrete block has left a tiny crack, allowing tears to pass through. I glare out of my bedroom window to the immaculately trimmed garden hedges outside, lit up by the Art Nouveau lamps. I don't really see the created illusion of perfection outside though, I see the girls. I was so incredibly happy back then. Life was full of promises, full of excitement and every single little outing was fun. It didn't matter whether it was shopping for vintage clothes with Alzy, going on an Art Nouveau walk with Ing or going on one too many nights out with all of them. Every single thing brought happiness. The full realisation of the emptiness I've been experiencing since breaks me. The only glimmer of hope I've had since then was our trip to Budapest, but that broke me even more. I haven't been excited since. I've laughed, sure, because let's be honest - cat and dog fail videos melt the toughest of hearts, but I haven't appreciated life since. I've been going through the motions (that reminds me of that musical episode of "Buffy the Vampire Slayer", I need to rewatch that), plotting on, day to day. How on earth will I ever get over losing them? Alzbeta, Ayat, Marieke, Karla, Ingvild and all the others - they hadn't done anything wrong. People grieve over a single loss their entire lives. How can I grieve all of them in just one lifetime? I don't have enough time. My stomach hurts from the sobbing.

A knock on the door.

"Liv, are you okay? I want to give you your space, but I'm here if you need me." I hear Balazs' gentle voice coming from the other side of the door.

"Come in." Those are about the only words I can utter at this moment. He opens the door and rushes to the bed, wrapping me up in that tall Hungarian hug of his I won't ever get tired of.

"I can't -"

"Shh, you don't have to say anything. Just cry, get it out."

So I do. I have no idea how long we stay in that hug, but time is irrelevant when I can finally - at least temporarily - release this pain. It is so unbearably hard, but relieving at the same time.

"I love you." He whispers and squeezes a bit harder.

"I love you, too."

Chapter 28

LUKAS

I'm still not used to the taste of cigars, but it has become a pleasant tradition. Mirek runs his fingers across the dark oak desk and stares at his whiskey glass. He's in one of his introspective moods.

"Lukas, I need your professional opinion on this. We've talked about it numerous times, but now that you've met all these people, I'd like you to tell me again."

I take a drag from the cigar - don't inhale, you've made that awkward mistake before - and exhale the smoke towards the matte black ceiling. The contrast of the light grey swirls and black background makes for an interesting picture.

"I suppose you mean the suspect list."

"Indeed. Am I still on the list?" A tense pause hangs in the smoky air.

"You are." I've learned that the best way to communicate with Mirek is by being bluntly honest. "Just as much as Basia is. You've been around Oliwia since this all started. Money and status can do strange things to people."

"But you do take into account that she's my daughter?"

"I've seen people do worse."

"Right, okay." He doesn't protest, I know he wants to hear

more.

"Oliwia said something today that stuck with me. She mentioned that in trilogies-"

"Not you too." An exasperated sigh leaves his tense lips.

"Hear me out. In trilogies in the final chapter it always goes back to the beginning. Now, I'm saying this because the killer or killers know a thing or two about Slasher structures. If that is the case, then let's go back to the beginning."

"Europea Halls?"

"Or the movie club. The fact that Saskia and Erik have been murdered makes me wonder if there's a deeper connection between Oliwia and this club that I haven't figured out yet."

"Does that make Jelena a suspect then?"

"Oh, absolutely. She's the one connecting factor between those siblings and Oliwia."

"But there were so many people in that club. Around thirty if I recall correctly." Mirek has a way of being intense without blatantly showing it. His tone and pace is calm, collected, yet there is an urgency to his delivery.

"And two of the previous killers did join in now and then." I add.

"Right, Lucija and Karel. Who else was there from the beginning who is still alive?"

"Oliwia is the only one I can think of. I have checked the list of attendees and over the past two years the number has drastically dwindled down. I guess the pandemic didn't help."

"But nobody except for Jelena that stood out?"

"No."

We both sit with our thoughts. I peer at the alphabetised bookcase on my right, as structured as Mirek's rationale. He picks up his crystal glass and takes a sip of the undoubtedly-

CHAPTER 28

expensive whiskey .

"You are still on my list too, Lukas. You've been around us the entire time and you know the ins and outs of this family by now." There's no reproach or threat in his voice, he sounds factual. "I mean, looking at it objectively. Because you know I do very much appreciate your company." A small wink.

"The feeling is mutual." I wink back. "And I understand why you'd think that. Now, for the other people I have met. I cannot see Balazs or Abelina being killers. Balazs tumbled into this entire thing purely by chance."

"Or *did* he?"

"How so?"

"Well, out of all the people my daughter could've met in Budapest, it ended up being him."

"Yes, but that was through those three friends she'd met on the ferry. I doubt they were in on it too as they all got killed."

"Fair point. It's always the nice ones though. That man is so soothing and kind. Call me bitter, but I don't know if I can trust him. Anyone who's been close to Liv has either been killed or been a killer."

"It makes sense for you as a father to be cautious. Completely. I am just saying he is not a suspect in my book."

"Might that be 'cause of your obvious interest in him?" A sly smile appears.

"My interest? Sure, he is good-looking, but I am a professional."

"The man is indeed beautiful, and I believe he has noticed you too, Lukas."

"Has he? I'm not sure." Why am I blushing? Stop acting like a kid. "In any case, I don't believe I am what he is or isn't looking for."

"You young people, so complicated. In my days we got married and worked on our marriage. You give up too easily. Or, in your case, you don't even start."

There is a lot to unpack there, but I doubt an aristocratic white straight man would get it. I've tried before, but always hit a brick wall when it comes to explaining what being aro means. Balazs is aroace, so I want to be respectful of that and not impose myself. Then again, maybe a part of him *is* interested? How would I even go about it? I know some aroace people do end up in relationships, but what would that look like? Do I even want that? The aro part of me can't picture it. Not the time, it's not the right time for this.

"And then there's Oliwia."

"She is still on your list? How could my daughter ever be on your suspect list? Have you not seen her PTSD attacks?" This is the first time I have ever spotted a hint of frustration in his voice. "Have you not heard what she's been through?"

"Of course I have, but you know I still need to remain emotionally detached when it comes to analysing all of this. Her attacks could be an indication of a personality disorder, leading her to kill without her even realising."

He scoffs. "Very unlikely."

"Very unlikely, but not impossible."

"How about your colleagues then? I know Jan was rather close to LeBeaux."

"He was, but he was also incredibly shocked when he found out about her."

"Anyone could feign shock. That detective had connections with so many people."

"She did, I do admit that. There are times when I double check my colleagues, cause the wariness in me tells me to keep

CHAPTER 28

an eye on them. I had never suspected LeBeaux, so I see your point. How about the Arms?"

"The guards?"

"Yes, they have access to all floors, all doors, you name it."

"But then why would they all have been killed that night of the massacre?"

"Someone could've gone rogue without the rest of them knowing."

"Someone who has a special interest in my daughter?"

"Perhaps. Whoever is behind this entire thing has some sort of obsession with Oliwia that we're not seeing. Is it money, jealousy, love, hate?"

"Or all of the above."

Balazs storms into the office without knocking. I am waiting for a lesson in politeness by Mirek, but before his appalled expression even gets the chance to settle, Balazs smashes the door closed and takes his phone.

"I'm so sorry to disturb you two, but you need to see this." He looks at me quickly, then stares at the floor for some reason.

Mirek and I watch a TikTok video of what looks like Jelena being drowned in the ponds of Ixelles. The killer is pushing her head down and even though the video is quite blurry, I can spot that there are cuts and blood on her face. Mirek looks away in disgust; sadly, I have grown accustomed to sights like these. Or desensitized rather.

"It's all over the news!" He is out of breath and in a state of fear, that poor man.

"Haven't you heard, Lukas?"

"No, I was talking to Mirek, I didn't -"

"Why wouldn't anyone in the office contact you? The police

are all over this."

A sinking feeling of deep shame hits me when I realise my phone is charging in my (current) bedroom. Absolute faux-pas. "My - my phone is charging."

Both men gawk at me in disbelief. "I know, I know, not professional, I'm sorry. What else did you see, Balazs?"

"I read on Bruzz that Jelena has passed away and that her mother was attacked too. She made it out alive though, she's been taken to hospital."

Mirek blows raspberries. "I guess that means we can cross Jelena off the suspect list."

Balazs looks at him in shock. "That's a bit tactless." He blurts out.

"Is it? I didn't mean it like that, but we've been discussing potential suspects. I apologise if that came across ill-mannered."

"Well, it did." Balazs definitely has less of a filter on than what I have seen so far. "Oliwia doesn't know. I was with her until now, she had a tough night, so I stayed with her until she fell asleep."

"That is very sweet of you, young man."

"She doesn't know about Jelena? Wasn't she supposed to video call her though the moment she got home?" I ask.

"She was, I think Oliwia somehow forgot about that, the PTSD probably kicked in. It seemed like it in any case when I entered her room."

"Should we tell her now?"

"No, Lukas, let my daughter sleep. It's been a long and intense couple of days. She deserves some rest. She will need all the strength and focus she has left. I imagine her walking back into Europea Halls tomorrow will be very challenging. Let her have this moment of replenishment."

CHAPTER 28

He's right. Balazs looks baffled each time Mirek speaks, maybe he's not used to more than three words at a time, but we're in his office, this is where chatty Mirek resides. Balazs nods at Mirek's suggestion, or order. "You're right, she deserves it."

He hasn't looked at me this entire time, so purely out of selfishness I direct my question at him. "Will you come along to the halls tomorrow, Balazs?"

Wow, actual eye contact, so he doesn't hate me after all.

"Of course I will, I can't leave Liv behind."

"This does mean you are putting yourself in danger."

"Listen, I've lost my sister. I can't lose her too. If there is any way I can help her tomorrow, even by physically being next to her, I will."

Mirek smiles for the first time since Balazs' unexpected visit. "You truly are an empathic soul. I appreciate you." Perhaps he does trust Balazs after all. Who knows.

"I agree." Fine, I'm not as eloquent as Mirek. "Very nice of you. I will be by your sides, too." A part of me hopes for a grateful look, but he only mutters a small "thanks".

"Let's all get some rest. My daughter needs us to be fresh too. Tomorrow is a big day."

Chapter 29

BASIA

Oh golly, how I have missed entertaining. My life has been so isolating and claustrophobic, it is such a pleasant sight seeing everyone around me enjoying their eggs Benedict. Louiza has done a marvelous job, yet again, with her breakfast delivery. The eggs don't taste as lush as they usually do, my stomach an inch more clenched up. The others seem to be hungry though.

I had a very enjoyable conversation with Abelina yesterday evening. We decided to let our children have a moment to themselves and bonded over the fact that being mothers is a much tougher job than people make it out to be. Especially when they have gone through unspeakable trauma. I believe she is warming up to me. I try to sound a bit less posh; quite the challenge, I do admit. At the end of the day, we're all humans doing the best we can. From what she has told me, I can gather she is a glorious mother. It shows prejudice holds no place in today's society.

Witnessing my daughter's deflated posture after finding out about Jelena's untimely passing was not an easy thing. I have seen it many times now, this look of despair and pain. She said she did see it coming when she woke and still hadn't heard from her, almost as if she wasn't even surprised anymore. Another

CHAPTER 29

death. One gets used to even the worst of things, the banality of it all. Oh - delightful sauce, I have to tell Louiza when she comes back.

"So what are today's events?" I ask, even though I know all too well.

"Can you stop sounding like that mother from "Saltburn", please?" Oliwia retorts.

"What is Saltburn, my love?"

"Nevermind, Mum. Anyway, Balazs, Lukas and I are heading off to the police station after breakfast, which is rather splendid, might I add." She jokes. It's her way of saying she's sorry. "We'll come home for lunch and then make our way to the halls." No jokes this time.

"How are you feeling about that?" Abelina inquires, a warm look of sympathy addressed to my daughter.

"I can't really put it into words. There's a bit of excitement, in a dark and twisted way, to get to the bottom of everything. Today I woke up with the hope of some sort of resolution, you know? Like going to a Gothic version of Disneyland." We all smile. I appreciate her trying to make light of a situation too hard to express. "Who knows, by tonight we could all be living our best lives again."

"It's giving hope." Balazs adds.

"It's giving, boo." She smiles back.

"What are you giving?" Poor Mirek, never one to catch up on the youth's slang.

"Final Girl power." We all laugh again, some coming from awkwardness more than anything else.

"So, darlings, whilst you are at the station I will make a quick pit stop at Auntie Jacqueline's."

"Whatever for?" Mirek looks confused.

"She's been utterly fearful about this entire situation. She asked me to come over for a spot of tea, so I can explain things to her. You know she doesn't do texts or calls, doll. I have asked Lukas for one of those policewomen from yesterday to accompany me."

"Mum, is that really necessary? Today? Of all days?"

"She is still family, Oliwia. She is old and out there on her own in that dire place."

"I would hardly call that loft 'dire', but fine."

"I will be back for lunch."

"You know how I feel about splitting up, though." There's a pang of fear in her eyes.

"How about we all go to Europea Halls this afternoon, then? All of us together?"

Abelina's posture stiffens. "Is - is that the smartest idea?"

"It isn't." Lukas speaks up for the first time this morning. "I believe it is best for Balazs and Oliwia to go together, the corps will join, too. The parents should stay home."

"Do I get a say in this?" Oliwia frowns at him.

"I'm sorry, you're right. What are your thoughts on this?"

"Eh, the same as yours actually, it's only that I don't like decisions being made for me. But yes, the parents should stay here."

Abelina seems relieved. "If that is what you wish."

Balazs agrees. "No need to put everyone in danger."

"Then why are *you* going, Son?"

"We've talked about this, Mum. I'm not leaving Oliwia behind. That's not even up for discussion."

Abelina throws her hands up in the air, raising the white flag. Like I said, it's not easy being a mother.

CHAPTER 29

As I take the plates away to put them in the dishwasher - we should get new staff in once this is all over - Balazs, Oliwia and Lukas put on their coats. We pause and look at each other, all of us. There's a false sense of security when the entire group is in the same room together. A small break from reality, even though Damocles' sword is still precariously dangling above us.

I'm the first to cut through the silence. "Please be careful, all of you. We love you."

"Love you too, Mum."

"Love you, Mum." Balazs adds to his mother.

"Love you -" Lukas starts, the words hanging in the room. We all crack up, the poor man probably can't wait to live his own life again. "Right, ready?"

"Ready." Oliwia nods, persuading herself.

Chapter 30

OLIWIA

I didn't expect to walk back into the exact same interrogation room I did when this all first started, but I can't say I'm surprised. Everything is starting to become cyclical. When we walked past Grand Place, I had another flashback of sitting down next to the Christmas tree with the girls, right after Alzbeta had passed. That was the first time I felt the surreal sensation of living in a fictive world, as if my life was too absurd to be real. A part of me wants to tell Balazs about that night, but what good would that do? I'd be living out the past once more, not contributing anything to this moment.

Ah, there they all are. Lukas is seated next to Jan and two other people from the corps. There's four of them in total, one being the new detective. A woman with long, blonde hair. Shocker. The Temu version of LeBeaux.

I glare at the water dispenser with a yellowed plastic cup underneath. Some things never change.

Chapter 31

ABELINA

Basia hugs me before stepping out towards the police car, on her way to her auntie. I stand at the front door, waving her out. How absurd, really, I only met this woman yesterday. Somehow being thrown into this tense situation made us bond quickly. She's hilarious without even trying to be and a little bit obnoxious too, but she means well. Most mothers do, I know for a fact I do.

Mirek stands next to me, a look of angst in his eyes as he sees his wife leaving. The policewoman named Britt made herself at home, eating one of the untouched eggs and sat at the kitchen counter, waiting for us to come back in. That is no doubt a no-go in Richie Land, but Mirek has kept his comments to himself.

So, now what? I doubt this guy will be talkative with me. He only chats with Lukas. He looks up at me and says, "Well, now we wait," and then he walks off into the kitchen. Great, this is going well.

"These eggs are, like, real good!" Britt shouts around a mouthful of food. Mirek looks like he's about to spontaneously combust, but holds it together well. "What are they called in English?"

"Benedict." He mumbles. "Eggs Benedict."

"Need to write that down. Always good to practice your English in Brussels." She grins, some yolk stuck between her teeth.

This is going to be a long morning.

"So, this place here is real nice. Who is the mastermind behind the interior stuff?" At least she's trying, I'll give her that.

"That would be my other half."

"The fun half?" She jokes, and I can't contain my smile.

"I mean my wife."

"Yeah, I got that." She looks at me and not-too-subtly winks.

A knock sounds at the door. Mirek and I instantly look to Britt. She jolts up and reaches for her gun.

"Could that be your wife?"

"I - I doubt it. She doesn't *do* knocks."

I want to ask why, but I refrain from doing so. Probably a posh thing. My palms are sweaty.

"The two of you stay here." She walks out of the kitchen and turns right, towards the front door. We can't see her.

"Should we -?" I signal to the kitchen door, so we can spot the front door.

"Let's."

We walk to the other side of the kitchen and peek our heads out to see Britt in the distance. She holds the gun in front of her and swings the door open.

It's him. The Killer, and he's holding a machete.

I instinctively grab Mirek's hand.

Britt fires at his chest, but it doesn't slow him down. With one aggressive swing he decapitates the cop. Her bloodied head rolls down and off to the side, before the rest of her body caves

CHAPTER 31

in and drops to the wooden floorboard. I want to scream, but Mirek puts his hand over my mouth.

He whispers, "the basement," and drags me to another door on the other side of the kitchen. I hear the killer's footsteps; he's running down the foyer towards the living room. He's on the far side of the ground floor. Good. Oliwia's words echo through my mind: we're not supposed to be the demographic.

Mirek and I sprint to the other door and move to the heavy concrete staircase, then down into the dark basement.

"I need to call Balazs!" I whisper, but Mirek is not having it.

"No time, be quiet."

Step after step, we inch closer to darkness. The humidity and drop in temperature make me shiver. We run past row after row of wine barrels and exposed brick arches filled with wine bottles. A wine cellar, of course. I'm not surprised. We duck down behind two large wine barrels at the end of the basement.

"Now what? We can't move here."

"I closed the door, he won't come in here. Visitors never notice the basement door."

That's comforting, as if the killer wouldn't have done his homework. I rub my arms, my body wasn't ready for this type of cold.

"Mirek, I don't feel good about this. If he comes in here, we're trapped like rats. We should run."

"We should stay put. Let me call the cops." His stubbornness is going to get us killed. Why did I even follow him down here? My shallow breathing makes it hard to think clearly. The trickles of sweat prickle my eyes.

We hear loud footsteps above us. If I'm right, the figure is in the playroom, where the pool table is.

"He's right above us, Mirek, we need to get out. Is there a

way out? We can run to the gardens."

"Shh, wait!" He puts his index finger in front of my mouth - the audacity of this man - and moves to ring the police. "Shit." A curse word? From 'Mr. Proper'? "No signal." I roll my eyes, of course there isn't. We're in a goddamn basement. My heart is pumping in my throat. I need to get out of here, with or without Mirek.

"So, what now? Mirek, seriously, I want to get out of here. You're setting us up for failure."

"Let's be quiet. We can wait him out."

"Wait him out? Do you *want* to get killed?"

Sweat beads are forming on his forehead. He might sound cool and collected, but he is as terrified as I am.

The basement door swings open.

I hold my breath, as if it'll keep me hidden. Mirek clutches onto my hand.

We have nothing on us. No weapons. I look to my right and see a bunch of old, cobwebbed wine bottles in the arch. I let go of Mirek's hand and crawl towards the rack.

Mirek gives me a "What are you doing?" gesture, but I ignore him. I'm not going down without a fight. I take two bottles and give one to Mirek. He might be a stubborn ass, but he's still Oliwia's father.

We peek between the two wine barrels we are crouched behind.

He's there. The killer is there. The slight ray of sunshine coming from the back window of the cellar illuminates the outline of the killer's frame.

He is walking towards us. There's so much power in those steps, it's beyond frightening. One arch at a time, he smashes the wine bottles with the giant machete. Mirek gasps in

CHAPTER 31

disbelief, tears pooling in his eyes. Not sure if it's about the wine or the killer.

Three arches between him and us.

I need to smash his head in with a bottle and make a run for it. I can do this. Balazs can't lose me too. Tears form in my eyes. *Think of Balazs.*

He's only two arches away from us now. I poke Mirek and show him my plan, he nods. A tear makes its way down his face.

I will not die. Not today, sir.

The calculated steps of the killer slow as he reaches the final arch. I can smell death on him. A mix of blood, rust and leather nauseates me.

He takes four more steps until he reaches the barrels. He knows we're here.

I jump up. I'm up, face to face with the killer. I had seen that mask in the news and Balazs described it to me so many times. But actually seeing it, the haunting features of it. This is how Balazs must've felt.

I smash the bottle onto his face. "This is for Szofi!" I yell out and slide next to the barrel past the killer who is visibly taken aback by the shock of the thick glass.

Mirek isn't following.

I can run, I can make it out.

Why is Mirek still sitting there? *Move. Come on, move.*

"Run!" He shouts at me from behind the barrel.

The killer directs his face to where the sound came from and lifts Mirek up.

He takes a pool cue from inside his overcoat and forces it down Mirek's throat.

The horrific gurgling sounds are too much. I hear Mirek's

neck cracking as the killer pushes the cue deeper down. I scream: "I'm sorry!" and run to the other side of the basement, towards the staircase. Arch past arch past arch, the yelping sounds coming from Mirek echoing deep into the cellar.

I reach the staircase. No more screams. I look back one last time. The entire cue is pushed down into Mirek's throat. His lifeless body is hanging onto the killer's hand, who is still holding him up.

I jolt out of the basement, into the kitchen, past the door frame and into the foyer where I scream again as I had forgotten about Britt's decapitated body.

The footsteps are back, this time more muffled, but equally scary.

He's coming for me.

I open the main door of the house and run into the gardens, towards the main gate.

It's locked. The gate is shut.

I glance up and notice the spikes adorning the top of the wrought iron gates. Nobody ever gave me the key code.

I can make it over, cuts or not. I *need* to get out of here. It's going to be painful though.

The killer bursts out of the main door and sees me immediately.

Now, jump.

I grasp the iron bars and begin to climb up. I slip down a bit, but quickly recover and continue climbing up.

Don't look back. I hear the killer running towards me.

I'm almost at the top of the gate, the spikes now seem sharper than ever.

The killer yanks at one of my legs.

"Get off of me!" I kick back and make him stumble.

CHAPTER 31

I tense my core muscles and heave myself over the top of the gates, the edges piercing deep into my hands and tearing my flesh. The blood flows down.

Don't give up, you're almost there.

I swing myself onto the other side of the gate while my hands are almost completely pierced by the spikes.

I cry out in agony as I pull them free and jump down from the top, then drop onto the ground. The killer stands behind the gates, flinging his machete through the bars.

"Not today, Sir!" I yell at him, ignoring the blinding pain.

I stand up and run down the graveled path towards a bigger road on the right. I look over my shoulder and see the killer is still standing on the other side of the fence.

I made it out alive. I actually made it. For the first time in what feels like forever I consciously exhale. I continue down to the boulevard.

Ping.

I scream once more before I realise it's my phone.

Balazs: *Mum, come to the Atomium, now!*

The Atomium? Oh right, that building with the shiny balls.

I signal a taxi and, luckily, it stops straight away. I shove my bloody hands in my pockets to avoid anything stopping me from getting to Balazs. How can I break the news to Oliwia and Basia about Mirek? It won't be easy. Those awful gurgling sounds rush back inside my mind, but there's no place for them right now.

I'm coming, Balazs. Hold on.

Chapter 32

BALAZS

Lukas, Jan and - I forgot the names of the other two - are diligently jotting down notes as Oliwia and I recount the past couple of days. I wasn't prepared for the questions about Szofi. It was like the hospital days in Budapest all over again, when the police came in every other day with more inquiries. Oliwia and I haven't let go of each other's hand since we started the questioning.

"Wait." Liv stops the others for a moment. "I received a text message."

We all know what that means. I bite my lower lip. "What does it say?"

"Hold on." Liv's hands are shaking. "I'm trying to -"

"It's okay Oliwia, we are here for you." Lukas replies.

"It's - it's an unknown number."

Of course it is.

"Well, what does it say?" I ask again.

"Let me read it out loud."

Unknown Number: *This is Abelina. Balazs isn't responding to me. I'm almost at the Atomium. I'm coming!*

CHAPTER 32

My heart drops to my shoes. What's going on here?

"Did you tell her to go to the Atomium?"

"No, why would I? I didn't text her." I glance at my phone, but I have no missed calls or texts. "She didn't call me."

"Cloned." Jan says. "Someone has probably cloned your phone. Try calling her."

I try to remain calm. I push the negative thoughts out of my head. *Not now.*

The phone instantly goes to voicemail. "No! It doesn't go through."

"Let me try!" Oliwia suggests, holds her phone to her ear briefly, then says, "I can't reach her either."

"The killer might have blocked all incoming calls and texts." Lukas explains.

"Then how did I receive her message?"

"No idea."

"What are we waiting for? We need to get to the Atomium, now!" I jump out of my seat and the others follow without hesitation.

We pile into the police car. Lukas, Oliwia and I take one car, the other three take another.

"Balazs, are you okay?" Liv is still holding onto my hand. "Can I do anything?"

"Not my mum. Please, not my mum." Tears steadily flow from my eyes. "I can't lose her too." I look out of the window and see the city flashing by.

"Hey, hey!" She shakes me. "Listen to me! Nothing bad has happened yet, we are heading there now. We can catch this bastard once and for all. Do you hear me?"

I nod, more to calm myself down than in conviction. "Right,

you're right."

Lukas turns on the blaring sirens and stomps onto the pedal.
We're on our way, Mum.

Chapter 33

ABELINA

"Are you sure you're okay, Miss?"

I fake a smile and wave off the comment. "Yes, yes, I'm a bit stressed, that's all." The blood is slowly soaking through my pockets. I try to hide it. I'm sure the taxi driver saw it when I was trying to call Balazs. The cold sweat on my forehead and the shivers running through my entire body don't bode too well. I need to get help.

"Should we notify the police, Miss?"

"The police, why?"

"Your hands. Is there something you're not telling me?"

"Just do your job and get me to the Atomium!" I shout out, a bit more viciously than I had intended.

He shuts up and continues down the big boulevard. Soon, I notice the nine massive metallic balls in the shape of an atom. The entire structure reflects the weak morning sun.

I almost thank the driver, but then recognise how ridiculous that would be after my outburst of anger, so I slam the door and walk up to the main entrance of the Atomium. There's nobody else around. That's weird, it being such a tourist attraction. It's far taller than I had imagined. I get a bit of vertigo when

I look up, the balls dancing into the winter sky. *Now's not the time for your fear of heights. Your son needs you.*

An acute pain hits my left hand, but I clench my jaw and push through it. I walk into the main hall and see an older woman with curly ginger hair looking up from behind her computer at the info desk.

"Madame?"

"Yes? English please?"

"I'm sorry, but we are closed today."

I don't get it. "But my son told me to come here?"

"Is he part of the event?"

"Excuse me, what event?" Stay polite, it's not her fault you're in pain.

"The private event for Marcolini in the top ball. It's their yearly New Year's drink."

"No, I have no idea what –"

"Then I'm afraid I will have to ask you to come back tomorrow, Miss. We open up at nine. If you want, you can purchase your tickets now, so you don't have to queue tomorrow morning."

"I – I don't need tickets. I need my son." I pull my bloodied hands out of my pockets.

The lady stands up as if in slow-mo, her face contorted with fear.

"Have you seen a man named Balazs? Long, curly black hair? Quite tall?" The desperation in my voice is impossible to miss.

"Miss, I would like you to leave. I can call you an ambulance if you –"

"I don't need an ambulance, I need my son!" I cry out. Where *is* he?

Then the lady screams, staring at something behind me.

CHAPTER 33

I turn around and look the mask straight into its black eyes. He's here.

"Let me in, please lady, let me in and block him out!" I shout, hoping she'll help me. I can't see her, as I've turned around, but I hear a clear clicking sound. The metallic gates to get into the escalators.

I rush off past the gates. The woman jams a button again to stop the killer from entering, but he blocks the gates from closing with his machete.

A neon rush of stroboscope lights wash over me as I start my way up the steep escalator to the first ball. Loud electronic music blares inside the tube. I run as fast as I can, skipping a step each time, so I'd get up more quickly. The murderer is sprinting behind me, closing in on the little distance there is between us. I shout for help, but my words don't stand a chance against that awful music. The flashy blues and purples of the neon projections swirl across the ceiling of the escalators, disorienting me.

I make it into the first ball with small windows in the middle. Some posters and info stands are spread throughout, marking the beginning of the museum. It's huge inside, it must be at least six metres tall. I scan across the room to look for any signs pointing to the top ball. Right, Oliwia told me it was a restaurant. I spot the sign I need and rush towards another even steeper escalator filled with neon lights and music.

The moment I step onto it, the machete swooshes past my left arm, the moving air warning me of how close behind he is now. I hold onto the railing because it is too steep to walk up without any support. I scream out in pain from the recent wound. The entire tube turns red - how symbolic. I see the second ball approaching as I keep moving.

Think of Szofi, think of Balazs.

My heart is beating so fast I feel like I'm about to pass out. My salty, dry lips make it hard to take in air. The killer hurls his machete at me again, but I duck down and miss its impact.

We fling into the second ball, way higher up. I spot the sights around me through the windows, but the height is dizzying and the entire room starts spinning. I close my eyes for a second.

Szofi's smiling at me. She's here with me.

I scream out as the machete pierces through my left ribs. The killer lets it sit there for a moment, surely relishing the pain I'm in. The dark blood spills onto the carpeted floor.

I try to stay up. *Don't fall down.*

Using my core for the second time today, I push forward, ejecting the rusty blade from my rib cage. There's blood everywhere.

Don't give up now. Get to that party. They can help you.

I somehow manage to walk to the final escalator, leading up to the restaurant.

As I enter the third tube, I am greeted by more neon. This time, however, there is also fog inside the tubes, making it nearly impossible to see.

I hold onto the hand railing. I have no idea where the killer is.

The machete cuts through my wrist, and I hear my hand drop, followed by a repeated wet thud as it slowly tumbles down the stairs.

I lose my balance and fall forward. I try to stand up, but the smoky fog, the neon, the music, the agony – they all make for a toxic mix of nausea.

The machete cuts through my bent over body, this time perforating my shoulder.

CHAPTER 33

I'm not going to make it. I can't fight anymore. It's as if a million little needles prick through my nervous system, stabbing me everywhere, all at once.

But Balazs. He needs me. I'm a single mother. I'm tough.

I pull myself up and wobble forward, again headed to the top ball.

A different world greets my eyes as I reach the final step. Classical music, people in tuxedos and gowns, champagne and chocolates everywhere. The views over Brussels are almost romantic, the light-green parks behind the structure and the distant Gothic church towers filling up the dense city.

I allow the full-on anxiety and pain to bellow out of my body as I scream: "Help!" My voice bounces off the curved walls.

They all stop and stare.

A moment of complete silence.

Then the yelling starts, the entire herd of people jolting to the other side of the restaurant, as far away as possible.

"Please, help me." My voice is weaker now. I hold up my wounded arm, still leaking with blood, to show how severe it is. A plea for assistance.

A man who looks like a security guard steps towards me.

"What happened to you, Miss?"

"The killer."

"The killer?"

The machete breaks through the guard's stomach, igniting more screams inside the monument. He has entered the top ball of the monument.

I shuffle towards the crowd, pleading for help.

Three younger women - about Szofi's age - take my arm and pull me deep into the far side of the restaurant. The other people make way and try their hardest to avoid me and my blood.

"Thank you. Thanks so much." I whisper. I'm fading in and out of consciousness.

The killer slashes his way through the crowd.

I can't believe my own eyes.

With an almost inhuman speed and force, he crushes through body after body. I lose count after twenty. A spray of crimson covers the room. Some try to get to the exit, but most don't make it. Some trample over other people's bodies in order to try their luck. Others hide away in a corner, biting their nails.

The classical music turns the entire slaughtering into a grotesque Baroque war painting. The diagonal lines of blood flying through the air inside the metallic ball create an insidious Golden Ratio of death.

Each cut, each slash brings him one step closer to me.

I tell the young women to run, but they form a human shield around me, protecting me.

Tears of gratitude and exhaustion block my vision.

Then it pierces through one of them, and the blood-soaked, rusty blade pierces through another's chest. She drops to the floor.

There he is.

No way out. There *must* be. My son, he can't lose me too.

The blade connects with my forehead. Everything turns black.

I'm sorry, Balazs. I really tried. I'm so sorry.

Chapter 34

BALAZS

"Why would she even go there? It doesn't make sense! She was going to stay at your place!" I shout out of frustration and fear.

"She probably thought you were in danger, boo. We're almost there, look!"

Liv points at the Atomium, stoically greeting us from the other side of the boulevard. Lukas drives even faster, the end goal in sight. The tyres screech as we turn left to park.

We're here. I instantly scan the surroundings to see if mum's around.

Wait.

Something isn't right. The hairs on my arms stand on end. I straighten my back.

A frantic group of people is making their way out of the monument. They're all screaming, faces filled with sheer terror. Some of them are limping, blood gushing from missing limbs.

So much at once. The sounds, the blood – where is my mum?

We step out of the police car. Oliwia whispers: "What on earth has happened here?"

"I think we both know."

For a moment, it feels like we're in the middle of an immersive theatre experience, the stampede of incoherent bodies bumping into us, some crawling on the ground. I spot a group of people standing stock still, no movement at all. Diverting my attention to another spot, I see an older woman, in a long, gorgeous black dress. She's pulling her hair out, bent at the waist and shouting: "My husband!" Several others are speaking, too, but most of them in French, so the sounds all fade into one sea of sickness.

Liv locks eyes with me. She knows what I'm thinking, surely. "We don't know, Balazs, your mum could be fine."

I know I have to move, to walk into the Atomium, but a part of me wants to stay here forever. At least now there's still a chance she's alive. She might've made it back - safe - to Liv's home. Here, now, in my head she is alive. There's no doubt she is. How could she ever *not* be?

"Balazs, we need to go." Lukas tries to sway me.

"No, sorry, I can't."

Oliwia strokes my back. "I get it. Trust me, I do."

She's squinting her eyes, trying to find a response somewhere within me, hidden beneath the surface.

"What if-? I can't, Liv."

"For Szofi."

That clicks. That is all I needed to hear.

Somehow, my feet lead the rest of my body to the entrance hall, past the group of people warning us against going inside. Lukas has brandished his firearm and stands in front of us.

A shaky old lady with ginger curls notices Lukas. She raises her hands above her head and pleads for something in French. I assume she's asking him not to shoot her. Lukas responds and the two of them get into a quick conversation.

CHAPTER 34

"What is she saying?" I wish I had paid better attention in French class.

"She didn't understand how Lukas knew there was a killer here. He asked her where it all happened."

"And?"

"The top floor. Or ball, whatever. Where the restaurant is."

"Lukas!" He looks back, surprised.

"Yes? What is it?"

"Describe my mum to her quickly. Maybe she's seen her." Perhaps we're wasting time, am I being dumb not shooting straight for the restaurant?

Lukas and the lady fall back into their frantic French ranting.

"So?" I ask Oliwia impatiently.

"She says yes. She saw her go up, but she-" She stops mid sentence.

"Tell me. Tell me, Liv!"

"Your mum hasn't come back down. The lady saw the killer rush past here, though, about five minutes ago."

She hasn't come back down. That sentence rings in my ears, on repeat, looped, a crescendo taunting me with what's ahead.

I nod my head. Lukas does, too. We all know it - we have to go up.

"That lady said there's a direct service lift, it'll take us straight there," Lukas states, his voice more frail than expected. "Come, this way."

The ride up takes what feels like an eternity. Flashes of memories soar through my brain, first of my mum and Szofi laughing on the sofa after I farted 'cause of those spicy peppers. Random. Next, my mum hugging me after I came out to her. Szofi buying me my graduation gown *way* too early, as if a part of her knew she wouldn't be there. My mum trying to understand Szofi's obsession with true crime. Mum and Auntie dancing in the garden to Hungarian folk music. All of us swimming in Lake Balaton early in the morning, way before tourists would arrive.

Szofi's death.

Her head toppling into her lap.

What if this morning was the last time I saw my mother alive? I said "I love you" to her, right? She knows I love her, she must.

I can't take this anymore. The muscles around my heart are aching with panic, in need of a release.

We make it to the top.

The laser in front of the door goes from red to green, signalling it's about to open.

The doors slide out – this is it.

A carpet of bodies glares at us. There's tens of disemboweled people, their severed body parts strewn all over the restaurant. Splotches of blood, splatters of intestine and scraps of flesh decorate the entire ball. Not one of us screams. I suppose we knew what was about to unfold in front of us. Still, there's this almost supernatural haphazardness about the way these people are lying on the ground or folded over chairs and tables. No human could've done this. No mere mortal.

I snap out of it and scan the carcasses in search of my mother. How is this even possible – looking for my own mum in what looks like a war zone. I search the carnage for any kind of movement.

But there's none. There's only stillness to be found here.

Then I see her.

CHAPTER 34

Her bloody body is sprawled out on top of the bar. On display. A sinking emptiness swallows me whole.

I've lost Szofi, and now my mother.

Liv comes in for a hug. I had forgotten I wasn't alone.

"Don't look, Balazs." She reaches for my face, attempts to pull my attention elsewhere. But I push back. I wriggle my way out of her hug and run to my mother's body.

Her face, her poor face. I never should've told her to come with me to Brussels. This is all my fault. She could've been safe with Auntie. I brought this upon her.

I kiss her cheek, the feel of her nearly-cold skin shocks me and I put my hand over her eyes, closing them with my fingertips. The semi-dried up blood sticks to my hand and I gag. I can't unsee this. All the stab wounds.

I'm so sorry, Mum. I hope you can find your way home to Szofi.

My heart breaks, only shards are left. My family is gone. I can barely see through the tears.

My right foot slips.

"Step back!" Lukas orders me.

"What? This is my mother, why would I step back?"

"Walk back, Balazs, there's a message."

"A message?" Oliwia sounds equally confused.

I take a couple of steps back, away from the bar and away from my mother. Now I get why I slipped. There's a message scrawled in the dark red blood staining the floorboard.

"What does it say?" Liv asks me.

It takes a moment to register. "It spells out Countess."

"Countess?"

"Yes." She frowns for a split second and then looks back up at Lukas, then to me. "My mother! She's next!"

Chapter 35

OLIWIA

The trip home is unbearable. I tried ringing my dad, but he didn't pick up. Neither did my mum. I'm hoping we'll get back in time. I try consoling Balazs, who stares aimlessly out of the backseat window. He's in complete shock. I want to be there for him, but I can't lie - my thoughts are with my own parents. Why won't they pick up? The smoky vision is setting in and my left arm is signalling me an attack is looming. The pins and needles in my arm together with the invisible claw scratching around my heart intensifies as we approach the estate. I can't even bear the thought of finding my mother the way Balazs did.

I deserve some sort of a break. Sometimes people whine about their exam giving them PTSD, which honestly does my head in. I hate how they talk about the disorder. They have no single clue what it is actually like, carrying this constant extra-condensed layer of anxiety. Not being able to breathe, to function, to live in this world. Or, on a good day, making it through all the triggers and then shaking in bed by the time I can unload all the unrest of the day. I shake myself to sleep, quite literally, every single night. I tremble until my body is too tired to keep on going and I slip into delirium. I need a break. I really do.

CHAPTER 35

Lukas pulls into the driveway. This time I'm the one who can't get my body to move. Balazs notices it immediately, of course he does.

"We need to find them, Liv. I'm with you." How can he find the strength to show empathy after he found his mother dead? Some people really are gems.

"I know. Give me a moment." I follow the inhale travelling from the pit of my stomach, enlarging my lungs and reaching my nostrils. I exhale and follow the air down my body. It's hurting, but I can still breathe. "Alright. Let's go."

Lukas, Balazs and I step out of the car and make our way to the main gate. There's blood on the spikes. I gear my head towards Balazs, looking for comfort.

"This doesn't have to mean what you think it does." Lukas whispers. Balazs can't speak; he opens his lips, but nothing comes out. He's trying, I know he is, but everyone has their limits.

I punch in the key code and we wait for the gates to open. The three of us stand huddled together, staring at the townhouse at the back of the gardens. My home. I stand in the middle, flanked by Lukas and Balazs who - surprisingly - each grab one of my hands. They're here for me, in their own way. *Don't let your guard down about Lukas, though, you never know.*

We walk through the gardens, towards the main door of the house.

It flings open and we all stop in our tracks.

My mother runs out. *She's alive.* She's been crying, an erratic stare catching me off guard.

"You!" She yells at Lukas, completely ignoring Balazs and me.

She sprints to Lukas and starts banging her fists into his chest and arms. "You lied! You lied to me!"

What is she on about? The claw scratches a little deeper.

"Wow, hold on!" He grabs her balled-up fists in his hands. She's shaking with anger and the tears continue rolling down. "What is it, Basia?"

"You told me you'd protect us! That we'd be safe in Brussels!"

Balazs rubs my hand. This *can't* be happening. My ears start ringing.

"Basia, please, tell us what happened."

"You *know* what happened. Mirek." She lowers her head, completely defeated. As if woken from a fever dream, she lifts her head up and locks eyes with me. "Oh, darling."

Lukas lets go of her hands and she moves in my direction. "Darling, I'm so sorry."

"Is he-?" I can't muster the courage to finish the sentence.

"Yes."

"What - what happened? *How*? The killer was in the Atomium, how is that possible?" She's fumbling over her words, trying to explain. "No! You're lying!"

I push her away and rush to the main doors.

"Darling, don't! Lukas, grab her!"

I move swiftly, but Lukas takes hold of me before I reach the doors. "Let go of me! Get your hands *off* of me! Where is he? Mum?"

She replies, but I can't hear her. The echoes and the ringing fill me, then take over. The tunnel vision grabs hold and my body quivers in disbelief.

The claws pierce my heart.

CHAPTER 35

I open my eyes, dazed with confusion. Where am I? What happened? The colours around me are blurry and there's still a faint ringing in my ears. I try to get up.

"Darling, stay there. Easy now." My mum caresses my cheek. "We're with you. You had an attack." I scan my surroundings: my bedroom. Lukas and Balazs are sitting at the edge of the bed and my mum is next to me.

Dad.

"Where's Dad? Mum, did I have a nightmare?"

She avoids my pleading eyes and turns away. "He's dead, Oliwia."

So it did happen. There's no way. Why him?

"Can I see him?"

"I've asked Lukas to cover the bodies."

"Bodies? Plural?"

"That policewoman didn't make it either."

"I don't care about her, no offense, Lukas."

"None taken." He throws me a gentle smile.

"I want to see Dad."

"I don't want you to see him like that. It shouldn't be your last memory of your father." She sounds calmer now. I have no idea how she does it.

We all sit in silence. My mind is empty. I cannot find the way back home. Nobody knows what to do or how to act, there's too much heaviness in the room.

"Can someone open the window, please?" I ask.

Balazs is the first to stand. A breeze finds its way into my lungs. "Thanks. I felt like I couldn't breathe."

He remains by the window. "I understand."

His mother is dead, my father is too. "Balazs, come here." I pat my hand next to me on the mattress.

"What?"

"You shouldn't be on your own."

"I'm not. I'm here, aren't I?"

"You know what I mean. You need someone to take care of you just as much as I do."

He sits down on the bed and plops a pillow behind his back. My mum is on the other side. Lukas stays in the same position, looking a bit out of place.

"Would you like me to give you all a moment?"

"We would appreciate that, Lukas." Mum replies. "Stay close though. Please."

He graciously walks out of the room and closes the door behind him.

"Mum, the killer left a message."

"What? What do you mean?"

"In the Atomium. Next to -" I look to Balazs for visual confirmation I should continue; he nods - eyes full of sorrow. "Next to Abelina's body. He had spelled out the word 'countess' with blood."

"Oh, dear. Horrid." She raises her shoulders and shakes off the visual; a lot of shaking things off has been happening lately. "Do you think it was meant for me?"

"Come on, Mum, I'm sorry, but who else?"

"Well, darling, you're a countess too."

"You are?" Balazs sounds surprised. I suppose it's not something I brag about on the regular.

"I am, but my mind just went to you for some reason. I mean, I hope not, of course! But after Dad- You know."

Wait a minute.

"Oliwia? What is it? I can tell you're thinking something."

CHAPTER 35

My mother perceives more than I give her credit for at times.

"Karel."

"The killer?" Balazs adds.

"No, Karel de Grote." They both stare at me. "I was being sarcastic. That's Charles the Great in Dutch. Anyway, of course *him*."

"What about him?" Balazs questions me. I'm being annoying, speaking in half sentences. Alright, be coherent. Now's not the time for that fragmented brain of mine.

"He used to call me Miss Countess. To tease me, you know, back at Europea. He was the one who started it. It caught on for a while, but I told the girls it made me feel uncomfy, so they gave it a rest. But he's definitely the one who said it first."

This is better than thinking about Dad. Focus on finishing this first.

"So there's a connection, you're saying?"

"Yes, Mum, I think so. There must be. Why else?"

"Darling, was there anyone else who called you this? Someone who is still, I'm sorry to sound so candid - alive?"

I chuckle. It's almost funny how nobody's left. Almost. "No, they're all gone."

"Who knows that you're actually a countess, Liv?"

"I'm not sure, boo, I mean - I don't exactly shout it from the rooftops, do I? I didn't even tell my roommates from the halls, let alone the teachers."

"Miss Raven knows, though." My mum adds.

"Who is she?"

"She's the headmistress at Europea. When we filled in the paperwork to get into the school, we had to provide very specific info, I remember now."

"And without our yearly donations, I doubt that school would still be afloat." My mother is beaming with pride.

"Mum, come on."

"What? I'm serious. Do you have any idea how much those rooftop renovations of the language block cost?"

"Wait, sorry to interrupt, Basia, but do you still donate to the school?"

"Well, no. We stopped once Oliwia pulled out. Why would I invest hundreds of thousands a year-" Balazs' jaw drops. "If my daughter doesn't go there anymore?"

"Motive." I blurt out. "That could be a motive. Not a good one, granted, but Lukas said it too. Very often it all boils down to money."

"This world would be a better place without it." Yes, sure Mum, easy to say when you're loaded.

"Right. You could be right, Liv. Who else knows?"

I signal both of them to come closer to me. I whisper: "What about Lukas, Mum, does he know?"

"Well, he's read a lot of police reports on our family, so he must."

"Lukas? Really? I can't imagine."

"That's 'cause you have a soft spot for him. A platonic one, before you scream at me." I wink. It's the first time we all have a faint smile on our faces. How? Don't ask me, perhaps a touch of normalcy is needed to brush away a reality too hard to fathom. Either we keep going and survive, or we think about the deaths and allow ourselves to feel and fall deep down into blackness. I can't afford to do that, for mum and Balazs' sake.

Lukas bursts into the room. We all look at each other awkwardly. Did he hear what we were talking about?

"The killer's been spotted." He says, out of breath.

CHAPTER 35

"What? Where?"

"By the Palais de Justice."

"Is that far?" Balazs questions.

"About a fifteen minute drive."

"Well, what are we waiting for?" My mum replies. "We're going. All of us."

"Mum, I'm not sure if –"

"*All* of us. No discussion."

Chapter 36

LUKAS

Basia is fidgeting with one of her golden bracelets. It's a bit distracting, but I shift my focus onto the road again. This could be it. We might be able to finally catch the killer.

"So, who spotted him?" Balazs asks me.

"It's all over TikTok. People are sharing videos of the killer walking around Brussels."

"Just walking around? In plain sight? And nobody has stopped him?"

"Would *you* stop an armed murderer in the streets?"

"I see your point."

"He's getting ballsy." Oliwia has her game face on. "He's taunting us, isn't he? How have the cops not stopped him yet if he's been sighted walking around?"

"He's outsmarted them."

"Of course he has."

"So far." I wink at her. "I won't let him get away that easily."

"Who rang you up, by the way?"

"Jan. Why?"

"Oh, nothing. I was just curious." She's hiding something. She probably suspects him, or me, or both of us. She put her walls back up after her PTSD attack and I cannot blame her. I

CHAPTER 36

don't take it personally. All I can do for these three people is do my job and show that I'm trustworthy.

"How much longer, Lukas?"

The shallow breathing next to me is quite telling. Basia's nervous.

"About two minutes. The rest of the team is on their way too, they'll be here in ten max."

I'm not scared like I was yesterday. It's high time to finish this. This has taken far too long, way too many people have died. We have all failed Oliwia; we, meaning the police corps. It never should have gotten this out of hand. I need to make amends.

Today is the day.

Chapter 37

OLIWIA

We step outside the underground parking at Place Poelaert. This is yet another square filled with memories. It's located higher than the rest of central Brussels, so it's a perfect spot to catch the sunset, overlooking the skyline of the city. You can see the Atomium, the Town Hall, the Basilica of Koekelberg, you name it. It's all there. Spread out before you to soak in the diversity of the capital. The girls and I used to come here for pre-drinks now and then when there was a party in the area of the Marolles. There's antique and vintage shops everywhere in this district. All you need to do is take the glass lift down from the square to the lower part of the old town and you're dropped in the middle of a quirky shopping heaven.

As we walk towards the edge of the square, we pass the large ferris wheel, which is basically a glorified tourist trap, but still cute. The imposing Palais de Justice is on our left. It was the biggest building in the world when it was first built. Ingvild told me that, obviously. Now it has become the symbol of the city in a self-mocking, surrealist way. The massive Neo-classicist structure has been covered in scaffolding since 1986. Over the years, renovations have been pushed back so many times that now there is scaffolding to support the old

CHAPTER 37

scaffolding. How meta. It kind of represents the city that way: the magnificent opulence of the building with its pristine golden dome, juxtaposed with the cracks that are hidden by the layers of scaffolding. The plaster that can rip at any given moment. It comes to no surprise that the killer was sighted here. He knows Brussels, so he knows the story behind this building. Justice will be served here, in one way or another, from either side's perspective. From the Atomium, built for the World Expo and our national symbol to the Palace of Justice, he's giving us a deadly grand tour.

"Keep your eyes and ears open, people." Lukas commands.

"Have you received any updates?" I ask.

"None. No more sightings. But judging by the tempo of his steps, he wasn't in a hurry."

"He's here. I can feel it."

I touch the outline of the butcher's knife in my coat pocket. We all grabbed one before heading out. Lukas wasn't a fan of the idea, but we were not about to head out unarmed. If he has a gun, we can protect ourselves, too.

We near the edge of the square. A bunch of teenagers are hanging out, taking selfies and drinking beers. They're all huddled up to fight off January's cold winds.

"It's beautiful here." Balazs says solemnly.

"It actually is, right? I know it's no Budapest, but there's something about Brussels."

"I wish I could've come under different circumstances."

"I'm sorry I brought you two here."

"What? No, don't go there! You did what you believed was the right thing to do."

"I was wrong though."

"You weren't. Don't do this, Liv."

"What are they doing?" My mum points at the group of teens. They're filming us. I had forgotten Balazs and I are known faces here. I haven't had any social media for months, but there's no doubt we're all over it. "How dare they? The impertinence!"

I want to calm her down, but there's no point. We're all on edge here. She walks up to the group. "Mum, don't. It's not worth it." She doesn't answer. She has a look of pity in her eyes. "It's okay, Mum, really."

"There!" Lukas runs off before I have a chance to follow his gaze.

The killer. That mask. It looks more worn out.

I'll never get used to seeing that mask. My heartbeat picks up.

Show time.

He's standing by the glass lift. A couple of tourists squeal and disperse. Lukas rushes towards the metal bridge which connects the square to the lift.

"Move, get out, leave!" He yells at all the bystanders. Most listen, but some film the entire spectacle.

My mum, Balazs and I follow him from a distance, not sure if we should let him handle it on his own. He's the one with the gun after all.

No, this is *my* fight.

I pick up the pace and decide to go for the bridge as well. Mum and Balazs are by my side, as they have been.

The figure is waiting patiently. He's spotted Lukas, but he's not moving at all.

When Lukas reaches the end of the bridge and faces the killer, I yell at him: "The head! Aim for the head!"

He turns around in confusion and shouts back: "What?" No, don't be that stupid, come on. You're a cop.

CHAPTER 37

The killer lunges in and stabs Lukas' back.

"No! Lukas!" We run over the bridge to help him out. He shrieks out in pain.

The lift doors open. The figure drags Lukas into the glass box.

We sprint towards the lift, but by the time we make it, the doors have closed. Lukas looks at me, eye wide with fear.

Balazs and I click on the 'open' button and smash the glass, but the lift starts moving downwards. Lukas' blood is on the doors.

"The stairs, this way!" I run past the bridge and onto the grand, zigzagging stairs next to the Palais de Justice. It goes all the way down to the other entrance of the lift.

I don't think I've ever run this fast. Balazs is beside me, but my mum is struggling to keep up. "Mum, hurry!"

We hear gunshots being fired inside the lift. The glass breaks on one side. People all around us are screaming. I look to the right and I notice more blood smeared on the glass. Lukas is wrestling the killer.

My heart is pumping fight into my system and I refuse to let flight take over.

Another gunshot.

I try to see what's happening whilst running down the stairs, but it's difficult to make out who's getting the upper hand. The figure is bent over and Lukas is upright, but there's so much blood on all sides of the glass lift. Whose though?

"Oh my days, poor Lukas!" Mum shouts out, audibly out of breath.

We reach the base of the staircase and make our way over to the glass lift.

Right on time, it's about to open.

"Knives!" I order the others.

We all pull our weapons out, ready – or I'd like to think so – for the fight.

The front of the lift is covered in blood, so we can't make out if Lukas is still alive.

"Go for the head or the throat!"

I throw a look at my mum and Balazs and they both nod, knives gripped firmly in hand.

Pling.

The lift doors slowly open. I am standing in front of it, the others right behind me.

Lukas.

His face is badly cut up, so is the rest of his body. I hear my mum gasping. It looks like he's still standing though. How? His eyes are glaring at me lifelessly.

Then it clicks. The killer is holding him.

He throws Lukas' body at me and rushes past. Lukas' heavy body falls onto me and I smack onto the cobbled stones, the blood dripping down his face and into my eyes and mouth.

I shriek in disgust.

"Stab him!" I manage to shout.

Balazs pushes Lukas off me. I'm disoriented for a moment, but Balazs helps me stand up again.

"Oh, darling, your silk blouse! It's covered!" Oh boy, be nice. She means well.

"Where did he go?"

"He was too fast, I'm so sorry!" Balazs replies.

"None of you got so much as a stab in?"

"I blocked. I froze, love, I have never stabbed a human in my life. Symbolically, sure."

They both cast apologetic glances my way. Of course he got

CHAPTER 37

away. He always wins.

Sirens sound above us, the rest of the corps arrives at Place Poelaert. Perfect timing. For once, can things actually go well? It's becoming comical.

I jump up.

"What is it, darling?"

"A text."

The three of us exchange glances as we all know who it's from.

Unknown Number: *Welcome to the Final Act, Final Girl. Europea Halls, now. No cops. Or your mum dies.*

Chapter 38

BASIA

I still vividly remember that first day. Mirek and I were so proud that Oliwia had gotten into Europea after all those selection rounds and exams. I had always known she was special, but outside validation was an extra welcome touch. She tried to play it cool, but I could see the excitement in her eyes. Mums know their children. When we finally unloaded the boot of the limousine filled with heavy suitcases and bags (no cheap plastic shopping bags, mind you), those handsome guards were waiting for us. Such gentlemen, too, carrying her entire new life into the halls.

She'd gawked and gasped at every corner, too taken aback to hide her enthusiasm. Now, my daughter is no stranger to luxury or delicate architecture, but her new home exuding this much refinement gave her the boost she needed. She'd been a bit lost when we first arrived in Brussels. Belgium is quite different to Poland, you see. The people, the food, the shops, the languages, everything was foreign to us. Oliwia had locked herself up in her room for months, studying French and Dutch. It had become an excuse for her to isolate herself, but she swore it was a way of preparing herself for her new academic year. I remember hoping this could be the beginning of something

CHAPTER 38

new for her. She merited friends, people who got her sense of uniqueness.

As we entered the second floor of the building, a blonde girl with exquisite green eyes smiled at my daughter.

"Are you the new girl?" She asked, no sense of arrogance, merely kindness.

"I suppose I am." My daughter stumbled over her words. Her English was still a tiny bit basic at that time, but I knew she'd catch up soon enough.

"Welcome! Want me to show you around? I know this place can be a bit much at first." How delightfully considerate of her.

My daughter's eyes lit up. A potential new friend.

"I'd love that!"

"Great, my name's Ingvild by the way, what's yours?"

Chapter 39

OLIWIA

After yet another Uber ride, we get out in front of the entry to Europea Halls. The entire ride was filled with silence, all of us coping with so much loss in one day. I do feel bad for not trusting Lukas at times, but it's my dad I keep thinking about, his - I can't even say it yet. I am appreciative that my mum didn't allow me to see him. Watching Balazs crumbling before me when he closed his mum's eyes was gut-wrenching. I don't know how the others feel at this very moment, standing in front of the main doors, but I don't have the mental capacity to be emphatic.

This is about survival and closure.

Balazs tried to wash Lukas' blood from my face, the Uber driver's face full of revulsion, but I refused. I need this war paint to keep me going. Every inch of my body wants to rest, to sleep off all the emotions, but I don't have that luxury. Mum protested when we set off without warning the cops, but what help have they been over the course of these past years? They'll know to come here, but undoubtedly a minute too late. I can only count on myself and the only two people left in my life.

I put my old student badge in front of the scanner and to my

CHAPTER 39

surprise, it still works.

"They never deactivated it?" Balazs questions.

"Apparently not."

"I thought they would've after we stopped our donations." Mum adds.

"Unless it's all planned. The killer obviously wants me here."

I push open the heavy dark oak doors and switch on the hall lights. My first glimpse into Europea Halls in years.

The entire weight of the world pushes down on my shoulders. I knew it'd hurt, but not this much. A crushing wave of memories floods me. I cannot let it overtake me, I need to look at this building for what it is: simply a building.

Balazs gasps. "So this is where you lived. This place is incredible!" He catches my eyes and quickly shifts gears. "Sorry, I didn't expect it to be so gorgeous. I'm sorry. How are you feeling?"

"There's no time for feelings, boo. I can't allow them in here." I wish I could ignore the pain completely, but I can't. This was my home.

My mum steps forward and strokes my back, she's with me. "So darling, what should we do?"

"You all still have your knives at the ready, right?" They both nod. "Good, then it's time for us to make our way to the library. It's quite the walk up there, but I'm not taking that service lift again." They don't ask any questions and comply.

We slide through the broad halls on the ground floor, passing the paintings I looked at every day before heading to school. All the deities, all the protectors that never protected us when we needed it the most. I swallow, but my throat and mouth are as dry as it gets. It's an obvious contrast with my sweaty palms. I squeeze hard into the handle of the butcher's knife and double check if Balazs and mum are holding onto theirs too. They are. One more painting before heading upstairs.

I don't remember this particular one. I pause and stare at it.

"What is it?"

"This wasn't here when I lived in the halls."

"A revamp?" Balazs asks.

"Maybe. Hold on." I step closer to the painting to examine it. Something about those eyes seems familiar. Like I've seen them before.

"Leviathan." Mum reads off the golden frame.

"Wait, what? Why would they put him here?" Balazs has a look of confusion mixed with anxiety in his eyes.

"Why? Do you know this god?"

"Yes. I studied him at uni. This isn't a god. It's a demon."

"A demon?" I try to find a rational explanation. "This must've been planted here. There's no way Miss Raven would allow a painting of a demon in these halls, especially after everything that has happened here."

"Do you think the killer did this, Liv?"

"Who else? What do you know about Leviathan?"

"I don't remember the details, but I think he was a sea monster from the Hebrew Bible. "

"A seraphim." My mum interjects.

"What?" Usually I'm the one with the answers, but now I'm lost.

"The highest angels. Leviathan was a fallen seraphim. He was always loyal to Lucifer and became a prince of hell."

"How do you know all this?"

"I had time to read over the past years, darling."

"Read about hell?"

"We all cope in different ways, don't we?"

CHAPTER 39

"I suppose so. Anything else?"

Balazs picks up where he left off. "He was seen as extremely envious, full of jealousy."

"You're quite right, Balazs. Which makes me wonder; why this particular painting?"

"There must be some kind of a connection." Clever Liv, might as well just shut it.

"Right, let's go up the stairs. Be careful. I wouldn't be surprised if the killer were already here."

As we walk up the grand wooden staircase, I can't help but instinctively scan for Ingvild's bloodstains. They're nowhere to be found, but a part of me wants to see them, to give me extra fuel.

We arrive at the landing of the first floor and I go for the light switch that connects up all the other floors. A sepia hue of majestic rays give us an ironically warm welcome. It may seem inviting, but I know better. I push back the different dorm rooms full of gossip and laughter from my mind.

We continue our walk up to the second floor, the tension and the heat rising each step we take. I can't speak for the others, but the closer I get to the library, the heavier my feet become. My body wants to keep me safe and walking up these stairs leads to the exact opposite.

The second floor awaits us with equally warm colours.

214.

My heart stops. The door to Ingvild's bedroom is open.

Balazs and Mum appear to sense the shock in my stance. "What is it, love?"

"That's - that was Ingvild's room." They both glare at the open door.

"Do you think we - we should go in?" The hesitance in Balazs' voice fills me with doubt.

"I don't know. Should we? What if it's a set-up?"

"It probably is." He replies. "But perhaps there are answers waiting for us." He might be right.

"What sort of answers? Darling, I don't believe we should frivolously walk about without pondering on the potential risks."

"Mum, we're here. This is it. We will face the killer sooner rather than later. This is the risk we've all taken by coming here." I need her to understand. "Whatever chance of closure we can get, we need to take."

"Okay, Oliwia, I'm with you."

"So am I."

We follow down the hallway, closer to the open door. I lift the knife up shoulder height. "Get ready, he might be in here." The anxiety that has been trying to come through swirls throughout my entire being. Dancing snakes full of venom ready to attack whoever tries to break me.

I step inside the pitch black room. I frantically scan for any movement, but I can't sense anyone being in here.

I flip the light switch.

The entire bedroom lights up.

I have a flashback of Ingvild, Karla and me sitting on the bed, talking about our upcoming exams as the light bulbs blind me for a second. The three blondes. A hint of a smile catches me off guard.

Then reality sets in. There's photos spread all over the carpet in the middle of the room.

We all kneel down to get a closer look.

CHAPTER 39

I should've known.

They're photos of all the dead bodies.

Alzy in the forest, Ayat in the limo, then some taken from what looks like the morgue. Everyone's here. About forty pictures, scattered around the room. A body count Jason Voorhees would be proud of. It's hard to believe I've lived through all of this.

My mum quickly grabs a photo, scrunches it up and puts it in her pocket.

"Mum, what-?"

"Your father, you shouldn't." She looks away, a tear forming in her eyes.

Balazs hovers above the photos of his sister and his mother. "How did it come to this?" He mutters.

We all go in for a group hug, still holding onto our knives, but needing a moment of solace.

"Show off." I grunt as I take one last look at the showcase of macabre photographs. This right here, this is the fuel I needed. Seeing all these people that were intrinsically part of our lives reduced to photographs fills me with so much anger and drive. "That's it. I've had it with this game. Let's run up to the library."

Chapter 40

BALAZS

Five more flights of stairs, apparently. My mum would be terrified walking all the way up. I wonder if she was scared up there in the Atomium. I know her fear of heights completely takes over at times. I still need to ring my auntie, I have no idea how I will tell her that her sister has died. It's strange she hasn't replied to my text earlier today. I'm glad she's back in Budapest though, at least someone in the family will make it out alive.

The sensation of holding the large knife in my hands is an odd one. In a way it makes me feel stronger, more prepared. However, it also heightens my fear and awareness that I'm not ready for this. Mum would've told me not to go into these halls, for sure. She would've put up a fight, but I told her how much Liv means to me. I can't let her do this on her own. She didn't deserve any of this. None of us do, but she's gone through the worst. In a way I wish her mum wasn't here, because I cannot even imagine how she'd feel if she lost her too. She'd be an orphan. I suppose I am, in a way. My dad left us when we were babies and my mum is gone. So is Szofi. All I've got left is my aunt and Oliwia. The pace of our stride shows we want this all to end, we *need* it to end.

CHAPTER 40

We are due a win.

Liv opens up the library doors.

I try not to show how in awe I am of the beauty around us. She's already looking left and right for a sign of the killer, but I am overtaken with the details of the grandiose room. The late Gothic stained glass, the paneled ceiling full of fresco paintings and the dark green reading lamps all magnify the opulence of this place. There's rows and rows of old, leather bound books. This is no ordinary school library, this is a space of knowledge and exclusivity. Much like Liv's home. I stepped into a completely different world the moment I got onto that private jet.

"Follow me, we need to go to aisle L."

Lovers' Lane, she's told us about this. The finality of the walk as we glide past the aisles bears heavy on my soul. I know we're about to find out who the killer is, there's no other way. I hope with the last strand of strength left in me that we will live to tell the tale.

Chapter 41

BASIA

"Here we are." My daughter says. Lovers' Lane, the aisle that connects up the whole story. The word 'countess' fills me with anxiety again, because there's a part of me that fears I have a potential connection to all of this without even knowing it. Was the message for Oliwia or for me? One thing I do know by now, none of us are safe.

"Now what?" Balazs asks.

"Now we wait." I'm not a fan of that answer.

"Why this aisle though, Oliwia? What happened here?"

"Well, I told you, students come here to make out."

"So what's the tie-in behind this aisle and the killer?"

"I honestly don't know."

"Let's browse through the book shelves then. It is paramount that we are all focused and do what we can to put a stop to this." To my surprise, Balazs and Oliwia immediately agree.

I let my index finger glide past the books in search for anything that could be of importance. Larkin, Larsson, Lawrence.

"Anything?"

"No, darling, how about you?"

"Nothing."

A sting in my chest reminds me of the state I'm in. I've been

CHAPTER 41

doing my best to remain calm and be there for my girl, but there are these tiny glitches in time when my body revolts and acts up. I notice the slight shake in my fingers as I continue sliding past the books. Lee, Leonard, Lessing, Lethem.
A stronger sting pulls me in.
   Leviathan.

Chapter 42

OLIWIA

My mum picks up the book. We all look at each other. This is no coincidence.

"The other books were alphabetised, darling. This one isn't. It's just the title. There's no author on the cover." She brings the book closer to Balazs and me. "It's rather heavy, too, which is odd for its comparatively small size."

We come closer and scan the cover. Besides the name printed in black on a dark red background, there's nothing else.

"Well, open it already!" I blurt out.

She does so. The pages inside are cut out, there's an iPad inside.

"What? How do I-?"

"Give it to me, Mum." I take out the iPad and switch it on. It doesn't ask for a password or anything. There's a video ready to be played. My chest tightens - are the answers I've been longing for on there? I can tell Balazs and my mum are equally tense.

"Hold onto your knives, keep looking around." I don't want the killer to catch us while we're distracted.

I press play.

CHAPTER 42

It's LeBeaux. She's seated in the interrogation room.

"That's LeBeaux." I explain to Balazs.

She starts speaking.

"Hello Oliwia. If you're watching this video, it means I didn't survive our confrontation at Europea Halls. I trust the others have kept up with the rest of the plan though." That awfully arrogant smile throws me. The others?

"You're probably wondering what all of this is about. It's about time you knew."

"Are you okay, love?" My mum whispers.

"I am, thanks, let's focus on this first."

"Did you know Brussels has the highest percentage of spies in the world? The criminal underbelly of this city is bigger than you could ever imagine. It's all about connections though, and money of course." What is she getting at? "We share something, Oliwia, you and I. We're family." Mum breathes louder than she usually does. "You probably don't know this, because Basia doesn't even know." I look up at my mum, but she looks to be just as lost as I am. "You see, Basia is my sister. Well, technically my half-sister." I pause the video.

"Mum, before we go on, is there anything you'd like to tell me? I want to give you the chance to -"

"No, darling, I swear to everything that I hold sacred. Nothing. I have no idea what this woman is on about." I know my mum, she's telling the truth. I hesitate to continue the video.

"Go on, Liv, press play." Balazs urges impatiently. I do.

"I was conceived out of wedlock. Your grandfather was a notorious womanizer and on one of his many aristocratic trips, he met my mother. She was Hungarian. He forced her to give birth to me in a deserted warehouse in Budapest." The birth certificates, they must've been legit after all. "She died there and then, in the most awful conditions you can imagine. I was left behind. Rejected like the scum of the earth." A harsh tone erupts from LeBeaux's mouth. "At 18 years old, I found out I was adopted. Nobody in your family, in *our* family - except for your grandfather - knew of my existence. Can you even imagine what that's like? Being stripped of any identity, my aristocratic rights taken away from me before I could even *speak*?" There's hurt in her voice now, the facade is fading. "Eventually, I met up with him. I wanted to get to know my father. I believed that was my birthright. I wanted to understand parts of my character that were darker than anyone around me. I hoped maybe he'd understand that side of me. He never gave me that chance. I think he was scared of me. Scared of the impact I could've had on his family, or - better said - his reputation. So he did what any rich coward would: pay me off." The evil smirk returns. "Millions, I am talking millions of euros. Well, if we're being precise, they were Belgian Francs back then. Anyhow, I digress. I was sworn to secrecy as a newfound millionaire. But the hurt didn't go away, my little niece." That last word cut through me deeper than any blade could. "I didn't deserve that kind of treatment, all I wanted was to belong. He had me left out in the cold to die, like he did with my mother. I wasn't having it anymore. So I used the money the smart way. I changed my name and entered the Brussels' Freemasonry." I have heard of the local Freemasons. I know architects like Horta, painters like Magritte and plenty of authors were part of it. "And it opened up so many doors. So many connections. You'd be surprised how many good people can be turned when given large sums of money. Before I knew it, I had built up an entire team. Policemen, coroners, guards at the halls, IT experts, you name it. Even some of your beloved friend-group." Karel

CHAPTER 42

and Lucija. Those bastards. "We all had our weekly meetings and martial arts sessions. I wasn't going to have any weak links, so sometimes we did have to get rid of some people." The way the killer got rid of Erik? "But you know what the worst part is, Oliwia? All that money still couldn't buy my son a spot in Europea. It was too late for me to get the education I wanted, but he should've been given the chances I didn't get, just because my name wasn't aristocratic." A son. The killer. LeBeaux had a son. This is all about money and family. Lukas was right. "So he became the ultimate fighter. He was so hurt by the rejection that he became the best fighter out of all of us. Way younger than Arms and some of the policemen, but so much more agile and eager to learn. He was going to get an education one way or another, so he chose to apply himself the only way he deemed right: becoming an unstoppable killer." Who is she talking about? Who's left? "So, without further ado, and I am positive he is listening to this as I am speaking: meet my son."

I set the iPad down, then look up just in time to spot the dark shadow at the other end of the aisle. Sure enough, it's the killer.

My curiosity is stronger than my fear, so I stay where I am and urge the others to remain behind me.

The killer takes slow steps towards us, his dark blue overcoat and dirty white mask becoming clearer as he passes the light bulbs of the bookcase.

This is the first time I fully take in his presence. The broad shoulders, the confident stride, the dirty black boots. And there's that mask. Somehow more demonic than I remember. The crevices around the mouth makes it look like a deformed, sharp smile full of shark-like teeth.

He continues down the aisle, closer and closer. I try to lower my heart rate, 'cause my heart is beating in my throat. I can't have an attack right now. I inhale through my nose and exhale through my pursed lips. Balazs and mum have both lifted their knives.

There he is. He stands still.

"Hello, Cousin."

That voice. I know that voice, muffled as it may be. Who *is* that?

"Fancy seeing you here." Think, *think*. "Here, of all places."

A rusty, large machete is lowered from one of his long sleeves. I sense my mother tensing up, ready to jump.

"Don't." I whisper to her. "Stay."

"Still don't get it?" He snickers. I can't reply. My mind is spinning, trying to work out the missing puzzle piece. "Let me help you."

The large gloved hand reaches for the mask.

I hold my breath, waiting for the reveal.

That voice though.

His strong neck bare, the mask slides up, showing his left ear.

Hold the knife.

A strand of dark blonde hair creeps up from underneath the mask.

One bright green eye pierces through me.

Then the entire mask is lifted.

Matej. It's Matej.

"What? How can you–?"

"Surprise!" He cackles like a madman.

"I saw you die, right here! You were stabbed!" I'm trying to

CHAPTER 42

make sense of it all.

"You *thought* you saw me die, Cousin. No no, Miss Countess, that was a fake knife."

"But you fell down. I saw your body."

"You didn't check for a pulse, now, did you? My mum snatched your hair and dragged you to the sofa before you had the chance to. Didn't you listen to her? *Coroners*. It's quite easy to switch bodies if you have the right connections." LeBeaux was his mother. We never did go to his place, he said he was too embarrassed to show his house. Only Lucija had been there. It all starts making sense.

"And money." I reply blankly.

"You would know about that, wouldn't you?"

"Why are we just standing here?" Balazs whispers. I ignore him - this is the time for answers.

"So jealousy, that's the motive?"

"You and your motives, really, so exhausting. No, that's not it. It's about acceptance, belonging. All these other people in Mum's team didn't really get it. That's why I had to cut them loose. This is about you and I, fam. No more loose ends."

"You mean Erik?"

"Right. Once he had served his purpose -"

"Which was?"

"The IT expert. He cloned your phones, he messed with Balazs' presentation. Nice to meet you, by the way, we haven't been properly introduced."

"A pleasure." He snarks.

"See, there, some people still have manners. He didn't have it in him to kill Jelena, so I cut him off. Fabrizio too."

"The guard?" My mum replies.

"Yes, hello Aunt."

"Kiss my ass." Wow, hello Mum.

"It's only us now. Balazs never should've been here, for the final showdown. Chaos and circumstance. It's time to finish this."

"Meaning?" I ask, knowing all too well what he means.

"Meaning you all die."

"And then what? You'll live happily ever after in jail?"

"If that means justice is served, then yes."

My mum pushes into my shoulder and rushes past me, flinging towards Matej with her knife. She lets out a feral scream. "Not my daughter!"

"Mum, no!"

Matej stabs my mum's stomach. The entire blade glides through her. We all scream while Matej laughs like an idiot. I run towards my mum, Balazs at my side, but before we can reach her Matej is jamming the blade into the same wound he'd just inflicted. A pale pink piece of flesh falls from her abdomen, followed by streams of blood. *Not my mum, please.* She is too stunned to speak.

I firmly grip my knife and shove it into Matej's shoulder, hoping it will loosen his hold on her. He yelps in pain. Balazs stabs him in the other shoulder. My mother falls to the library floor, a puddle of blood forming around her. I stab him again, and again. He's not getting away this time. Balazs follows suit.

An aggressive roar bursts out of Matej's chest. He swings his machete at Balazs, slicing deep into his arm. His knife drops to the ground. "Balazs!"

I hear a faint sigh come from my mother and I duck down to check on her. "Mum! Mum!" I grab her by the shoulders and pull her against the bookcase, so she can at least sit down. A grimace full of agony is resting on her lips - it breaks my heart.

CHAPTER 42

Balazs is fighting Matej next to us, punching him with his bare fists. I want to help, but my mum - I can't be everywhere at once.

"Kill him, darling." She coughs up blood. "For all of us." We both start crying.

"Stay with me, Mum!" I cannot possibly lose her too. I can't.

"Go, finish it." She can barely speak. She slaps herself in the face, shocking both of us. "So I stay awake." A small grin, there's still some fight left in her. She looks down at her bloodied stomach. "What an utterly pedestrian way to die." She winks at me.

"Don't! Don't say that."

A cut to the leg drops Balazs to his knees.

"Save him."

I scream out of pure frustration with the impossible choice ahead of me. I slap my mum's face. "So you stay awake." I turn back to Matej and run towards him, knife in hand.

Matej pulls Balazs by his long curls into the next aisle. I match Matej's speed and plunge the knife into his back. He tilts his head up towards the ceiling: "You bitch! We're family!"

He pulls his body off of my stained blade and pushes a wooden bookcase over Balazs. A loud thud sounds as it crashes onto him, the books flying from the shelves. Balazs shouts for help. He's restrained from the waist down. But he's alive. He's still here. "Kill him, Liv!"

They're counting on me. *I'm* counting on me.

Matej limps away from me. The hunter becomes the chased. No more chase scenes, at least not the way he wanted. I'm done running. I follow him down to the main hall of the library. The evening sun casts its tinted rays through the stained glass. The dark, colourful scene is set. Darkness meets light.

Look at that pathetic lump of a supposed human being. "All that training, huh Matej, and for what?" He stops and turns around to face me.

Here we are, killer versus killer. I've done it before, I can do it again. We stand in the middle of the hall, surrounded by sofas, books and reading desks.
"You know what I loved the most?" He asks, full of arrogance.
"What?"
"Watching Karla squirm. She did put up a good fight, I have to hand it to her."
"You bastard!" I jump at him, jamming the blade into his chest. The blade isn't going deep enough though, bullet proof vest, no doubt. He grins and jabs the machete deep into my intestines and I scream in anger and defeat. I twist my blade into the side of his neck, blood spraying my face. His eyes start to roll up, briefly. We fall onto the floor, wrestling, challenging each other's strength. We roll over the wooden floorboard, banging into desks and sofas, blades flying through the air, into flesh. Two more gashes in my stomach. One in his ribs. Blood covers both of us now. I'm not sure which of us has lost more blood. All I know is I've been through this pain before, multiple times, and I can make it out again. He's weak, I'm not. I've proven that, time after time.

I'm the Final Girl.

Matej squeals as I stab into his crotch. I give it a good twist and he lowers his guard; I'm on top of him. I bite down the pain, my body is shaking.

He coughs up thick drops of blood. "Dominatrix much?" He smiles, his teeth bloodied. I've got him, he's got nowhere to go.

CHAPTER 42

The head. Always go for the head.

I lift the blade above my head, ready for the final blow. "Say hi to your mum."

He swings the machete sideways, sinking it deep into my ribs. I fall over in torment, my insides producing outlandish sounds and movements. He makes his way back on top of me.

"Kinky. Guess it runs in the family. Lucija and I had some killer sex, too, way back when."

I hold back the tears, I cannot let him see how much pain I'm in. But the signs are there. The tunnel vision is back in full force and my heart feels strained. I'm the one who coughs up blood this time.

"Come on now, I thought you were stronger than that!" He plows the machete into my stomach and twists it. I cry out. "Two can play that game, *boo*."

"Balazs, Mum!"

"Liv, hang in there!" Balazs shouts back. Not a word from Mum.

I'm losing my vision. Black spots block my eyesight. I try to raise my knife, but Matej pushes it back down. "No, no, no, don't even try. Sometimes the Final Girl doesn't make it out alive, you know?" I can tell by his voice he is hurting too. I can see beyond the mask.

"They mostly do, though." I grin. I won't show weakness. What's his? Then it hits me.

I kick him in the groin, he drops down to the left of me, more screams. "See?"

We both lie there, out of breath, smeared in blood. This is going to be a fight 'til the finish. The ringing in my ears amplifies. *Stand up, come on.*

I latch onto one of the desks next to me and pull myself up, knife at the ready. Matej hasn't moved. I tower over him, one leg on either side of him. He doesn't move, his eyes are rolling upwards again. *Time for you to die.*

I grip the knife in both hands and bend over in the direction of his head. He locks eyes with me and stomps his foot into my stomach, sending me somersaulting over him, landing on the floor yet again. We both roar, equally enraged. This time, he stands up before me. My body feels blocked, jammed inside itself. I can't move. He stands next to me and pulls me up by my shoulders. Then he gets behind me. I want to wriggle free, but my body isn't cooperating. I'm out of strength.

The machete is pushed against my throat. Tears drip down my face, I know what this means. I had him, I *almost* had him. *Don't give into the pain.*

"Any final words?"

I close my eyes. If this means the end and my mum and Balazs get to live, so be it. Sometimes the Final Girl needs to sacrifice herself. I'm okay with it. I'm actually at peace with it. All tension leaves my body.

"Not."

I open my eyes and scan the room. It's my mum.

"My."

She runs through the hurt, towards Matej.

"Daughter!"

She throws her entire body at him, making me spin and drop to the floor. Mum holds firmly onto Matej and the impact of the hit causes the two of them to fly towards the stained glass window. The machete falls down next to me.

"Mum, no!"

But it's too late.

Mum and Matej burst through the multi-coloured glass,

CHAPTER 42

crashing into the air outside. I crawl towards the window pane and see the two of them holding onto each other, plummeting down seven floors.

There's a moment of silence. A moment when the world holds its breath and tries to find something or someone to believe in. The dark green, red and blue shards of glass float into the library. The reflection of the sun creates a mirage of a Cubist looking painting through the pieces of glass. There's an odd sense of beauty hanging in the air.

Then a loud crash snaps me out of it.

I look down and see their bodies splattered on the concrete path. Their limbs are stretched in unnaturally grisly ways.

They're both dead.

"Liv!" A cry from a couple of aisles back reminds me Balazs is still stuck. I crawl to him, one slow movement at a time. "I'm coming."

I drag myself closer to him, further away from my mum's lifeless body. From Matej.

Then I spot him, trying to push himself out from underneath the bookcase.

"Did you get him? Is he dead?"

I nod, more tears streaming down. "I'm an orphan now."

Chapter 43

EPILOGUE: OLIWIA

Balazs' auntie wraps her arms around me. She can't speak English, but her eyes tell me she's proud of me.

The last four months have been a whirlwind, to say the least. The police, as per usual, arrived a couple of minutes too late. At least they lifted the bookcase Balazs was stuck under, because by that time I had passed out. We spent the following several weeks at the hospital. An odd sense of familiarity after everything that had gone down in Budapest. Balazs was less injured than me, but he decided to stick around when I was still in recovery. Thanks to my parents' solid hospital insurance, we had the entire suite to ourselves. It became our temporary home. Another one. Something about the hospital felt different this time around though. I didn't wake up every other second in hot sweats, fearing the killer would be there. The loose strings have been cut.

It's over.

The grieving only truly started after we had done all of the funeral planning for my mum, my dad and his mum. Setting up a triple funeral, two for my parents in Brussels and one for his mum in Budapest was beyond difficult logistically and - more importantly - emotionally. My parents' ashes were spread out

CHAPTER 43

in the gardens of our estate. Abelina's body was buried high up in the Buda hills.

Once we were patched up enough to wobble back into the world after all that planning, Balazs and I stayed at my home for a while. It was too painful though, too many memories. I didn't want it, but I came into a lot of money after the passing of my parents. Legislation and legal matters were the last thing I wanted to think about, so I hired my dad's accountant to make sure both Balazs and I would have enough to last us a lifetime. Balazs wouldn't hear of it at first, but he's my found family. How could I *not*?

We discussed for a long time how to continue, where to build a life again. One thing we agreed on: we wanted to stay together. Grieving is less isolating when done together. Eventually, we decided to buy a house on the Buda hills of Budapest. I know, there's history there too, but there's something about that city. That's where I felt hope. Where I met Balazs. Where *his* home is. So why not make it ours? His auntie was hesitant to move in with us, at first, but once she saw the place, she didn't have to think twice.

So, what's next?

The Chain Bridge.

I haven't been able to stomach walking over it since we moved, but today feels different. Perhaps it's cheesy, but I'm someone who believes in symbolism and signs. That bridge was the connection between me, dealing with loss, and what life could look like on the other side - the Pest side. Karla died on that bridge. I wasn't ready to cross it. This morning though, I woke up to George Ezra's "Budapest" on my Spotify list. I had never played the song before nor am I a particularly big fan of his, but when it started playing the moment I woke up, I knew it meant *something*.

So here we are. Balazs is holding my hand and gives me one of his warm smiles.

"You've got this, Liv. I'm right beside you."

I glance back at our house on the hills, overlooking the entire city. We did well. Balazs' aunt winks at me once more and gives me a thumbs up. I imagine Mum, Dad, Karla, Ing, Marieke, Ayat and Alzy are there too. I'm not leaving them behind, but I am coming home back to my own body.

I look at the lions without tongues at the beginning of the bridge. A white ferry crosses the Danube in the distance.

I'm ready.

Let's walk.

About the Author

As someone who grew up in the 90s, Alan Shivers fell in love with the campy, MTV-era type of slashers. He mixes these 90s elements with modern European city vibes in his trilogy Europea Halls.

Next to his love for slashers and all things horror, Alan loves architecture, his Romanian stray dog, meditation and learning different languages.

He is based in Brussels, Belgium.

Subscribe to my newsletter:

✉ https://mailchi.mp/b57ece14816e/europea-halls-trilogy

Also by Alan Shivers

I have recently started up a Facebook group called "Queer Horror Books". If you'd like to support queer authors who write queer horror, please join in and have a look at our discount events and interviews!

Follow me on Social Media:
  AlanShiversAuthor on Instagram & TikTok
  Alan Shivers - Slasher Author on Facebook

Made in United States
North Haven, CT
11 May 2024